WALKING MOUNTAIN

A novel of the Frank Slide

by Terry Cassidy

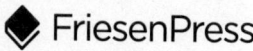 FriesenPress

Suite 300 - 990 Fort St
Victoria, BC, Canada, V8V 3K2
www.friesenpress.com

Copyright © 2015 by Terry Cassidy
First Edition — 2015

All rights reserved.

No part of this publication may be reproduced in any form, or by any means, electronic or mechanical, including photocopying, recording, or any information browsing, storage, or retrieval system, without permission in writing from the publisher.

Originally published by Novel Promotions, Penticton, BC 1997
ISBN 0-9682052-1-6

ISBN
978-1-4602-7068-4 (Hardcover)
978-1-4602-7069-1 (Paperback)
978-1-4602-7070-7 (eBook)

1. Fiction, Historical

Distributed to the trade by The Ingram Book Company

Walking Mountain is a work of fiction, and the main characters are imaginary, though Laura Freeman is based on a survivor of the slide, as is Lillian Clark. The main events are depicted according to factual accounts. An important source is *Turtle Mountain Disaster* by Frank Anderson (1986). Many fascinating individual stories came from the slide, but this work contains only those which might reasonably be seen by the two main characters.

The cover photo of Turtle Mountain is used by permission of the photographer, Dr. Paul Jerry of Athabaskan University.

Chapter I

"Mr. Delaney, sir, please, there's a letter for you." Burt Delaney had been staring into the big stone fireplace in the parlour, and he swung around. Young Lillian Clark, the maid in the company boarding house, stood in the door of the dining room. She was only two years younger than he, but so slight, so pale, that she seemed thirteen.

"Oh, hello, Lillian. Just warming up. But it's been a nice day, hasn't it? Almost spring."

She blushed, and did not reply. Seeing that she was not going to venture past the dining room door into the parlour, he stepped over to take the letter from her hand. It was franked in Macleod, though the handwriting would have told him that it was from Aunt Jo. Lillian remained rooted to her spot. He smiled. She smiled back and stayed exactly where she was.

Turning his back would be rude. He tore one corner from the envelope, then slid his finger along to open the top. When he pulled out the sheet of paper, another envelope, this one folded in three, came with it, falling to the floor. Lillian quickly bent to pick it up, unfolded it, and used both hands to flatten it. When she handed it to him, he saw the United States stamp and the printed "Delaney, General Delivery, Minneapolis" on the back. He glanced sharply at Lillian, but she seemed to be looking over his shoulder at something on the ceiling. Her head had to tilt considerably, for she was a foot shorter than his five foot ten. "Thank you, Lillian." It had the same effect as shaking her; she blushed again and whirled back into the dining room, right through it and into the big kitchen.

The gloomy second floor hall of the boarding house had only one narrow window at the west end, and now that the spring sun had dropped below the crest of the mountain, hardly any light penetrated the yellow gauze curtains. Burt pulled the big skeleton key with its wooden tag from his pocket, and crouched to get it into the keyhole to his room, Number 23. Once the bolt was turned, he pressed on the thumb latch to open the door, a raw squeak of hinge telling him he was home. A little rectangle of cardboard on the door announced "Mr. Burton Delaney" to the world, but a visitor would need a candle or a lantern to read it. There were no visitors, nor had there been in the ten months he had been living in the room. It would be ten months tomorrow, he corrected himself, from June 22, 1902 to April 22, 1903, ten months of the two years he'd calculated.

His room had more light, for the window faced north, that side of the valley still shining with reflected light. He could look right past the little town to see the great square ramparts of the big mountain that dominated the town from the northwest. When he'd arrived last year, Mrs. Hallam, the boarding house manager, had offered him the choice of 22 or 23. Twenty-two was a little bigger with a wardrobe in the corner, but 23 had better light. Also, the window of 22 faced the mine entrance, less that half a mile away, and at that distance there was no mountain to be seen unless you knelt down and craned your neck to look up. From 22, all you could really see was the track spur, the two bridges where the creek joined the river, and the little cluster of buildings across the river, the tipple where the coal poured into the big railway ore cars. Even then, before his first shift, he'd known that when he was out of the mine, he'd want it out of his sight and his mind. So he lived in 23, a room barely eight feet wide and about twelve long.

The bed was made of two-by-fours with a web of rope supporting a mattress of felt and cotton waste. Last November and December, he'd grudgingly yielded up part of his wages to buy, successively, two good wool blankets, and finally a buffalo robe. The robe was big enough to go under the mattress and right over the blankets. All the rooms on this floor were far distant from the big cast iron range in the kitchen and the stone fireplace in the parlour.

On the other side of the room an upright plank defined his closet space, a curtain of faded pink velvety material hanging from brass rings to cover a rough set of shelves and a few hooks on the wall. There had been another curtain of the same material on the window, but, eager for light, he had taken it down. Behind the closet curtain his possessions hung on the wall or rested on the shelves. On the floor, in a canvas sack, were his work clothes, heavy canvas pants, boots, a black cotton shirt, and a sweater, once red. His lamp stood on the floor beside the sack, with a broad brimmed hat.

Some of the men on the day shift were arguing that these soft felt hats were useless, that they should have helmets like firemen. That had been one of the issues in the big strike over in Rossland two years ago. Though the miners, the Western Federation of Miners, had lost the strike, some hard rock mines were starting to supply helmets. Not coal mines, though—the WFM had been forced to leave coal mines to the UMW, the United Mine Workers, and the UMW wasn't as tough on owners. But no union existed at the Canadian-American Coal and Coke Company here in Frank. In the two years it had been worked, the mine had no trouble getting workers, for times were rough in the Territory since the collapse of the cattle empires a few years back. No matter, Burt reflected, another fourteen months and he'd have the savings he needed for Aunt Jo and Jimmy.

He used a safety match to light the coal oil lamp, turning the wick down to keep it from smoking. The letters were in the slash pocket of his black woollen pea jacket, and he placed them beside the lamp on the small table. The one with the US stamp went to one side; Jo's letter first.

Her writing was half printing, in a heavy black lead pencil that smeared under his thumb. She must have written it in the kitchen, for there was an oily brown smudge about half way down. Poor Aunt Jo, she didn't get much time out of the kitchen of that Macleod boarding house. He moved the letter under the yellow glow of the lamp.

> Dear Burton,
>
> You'll excuse the rough note, but I'm forever busy as you know. This letter came from your Pa, my brother. Not opened, you'll see, but he told me part of what's there.
>
> Lord knows you have a mad on for him, and there's many wouldn't blame you one bit. But I know him pretty good. There's not that much harm in him that it would hurt you to think about what he's saying. You answer him how you will, but do answer.
>
> Jimmy is riding whenever he can, mostly screws from the stable that he combs free, but sometimes a good animal. Not as tall as you at that age, but his legs will go shooting out one of these years.
>
> You be careful at that job. I don't think it's natural to work in a place like that, but you're old enough to know your mind. Just take care. If they close down for a time, be sure to come here.
>
> Your loving Aunt Jo

His pocket watch in the bright nickel case glinted as he moved the lamp back. Twenty past six o'clock, and supper was six-thirty sharp. In fact, if you had an appetite (and what coal miner doesn't, he thought) it was wise to get to the big dining room early, to sit as close as possible to the end of the long table, the end nearest the kitchen from which the big bowls would be passed. Tuesday, elk stew and spuds for sure, and about thirty pounds of elk would be chewed within fifteen minutes by the twenty-four residents. Although half the people in the house were miners, he was the only one on the maintenance shift. The day shift men would be coming in any minute, dropping their lunch buckets in the hall and scrambling for the best seats on the benches.

Coal dust would hang in the air over the plates of stew, and there would be no talk, just grunts and gestures for the salt or the spicy brown sauce Mrs. Hallam put on the table.

The house was owned by the mine, but some of the residents were railway men, getting ready to build the new spur from Lille. Most of the construction labourers lived in the camp east of town, with four staying here. Two bank clerks found the house cheaper than the hotels along Dominion Avenue, and there was a family of four who found it quieter. The family could afford to get to the dining room later, as Lillian would bring them plates directly from the kitchen. No one objected; you could scarcely ask children of eight and ten to fight miners for their share of food.

While he was locking his door, he heard the rush of feet below, and knew he had tarried too long. The dining room table was three-quarters full by the time he got there. He stepped over the bench and sat beside Karl Grafton, completely black, with his coat puffing out small clouds of coal dust every time he moved enough to wrinkle the cloth.

Two rows of black faces, eyes startlingly white, turned to the kitchen door. It swung open, and Mrs. Hallam strode to the table with a huge steaming bowl, followed by Lillian struggling under the weight of another bowl. "Clunk", and the first bowl was off down the far side. The second bowl hit the table three seconds later, and lost even more ground with the third man on Burt's side, a notoriously fussy eater, who paused at least three more seconds selecting his second piece of elk. The bowl reached Burt with, miraculously, two large pieces of elk still in it. The potatoes made their way down the table with more grace.

"You're Mr. Delaney, aren't you?" Burt was caught with a large and, as it turned out, gristly, bite of meat in his mouth. He turned to see the mother of the two young children smiling at him. He nodded, tried to chew, and realized that he must look foolish. He pointed to his mouth.

Her smile widened, but not to a laugh. "Don't worry, I caught you unawares. It's not the best table for conversation, is it?" He followed her eyes up the table. Two rows of heads were bent almost to their plates, black necks stretched out, no sound but the scraping of spoons. He chewed three more times, quickly, then forced himself to swallow.

"I'm sorry, ma'am. That was..."

"Please don't apologize. You're a miner too, aren't you?"

"You mean why am I clean? I work the midnight shift, on maintenance." More than anything else, this was why he liked his shift, the unhurried bath he could have in the morning before tumbling into his bed.

"You're awfully young to be working inside that mountain."

Seventeen wasn't that young. There were some fifteen-year-old boys on days. "Only temporarily, ma'am. Another year and two months and I'll have my stake." Why was he telling her this? She looked concerned, motherly. Not like his mother, the dignified woman in the browning tintype he kept to boost his always fading memory. Ten years, next month, May 1893. Suddenly, looking at this woman, he had a flash, a memory of his mother a week before her death, wasted, thin, white, nothing like the picture upstairs. And his father, standing there, looking down at her, looking so weak and helpless. His father <u>was</u> weak. Burton Delaney had spent much of the next ten years realizing that, and growing in his own determination to be strong.

"Where are your people?" He realized that he'd been staring at her as if inviting her to go on with the questioning. Who were his people? Was it his father, in Minneapolis with his new wife, that Grace, who had just casually drifted into their life and left with his father and his sister, picked them up like an eagle getting a fish out of the river, hardly a ripple left where he and the baby stayed, stunned? Was that grouping, Mr. and Mrs. James Delaney, Mr. Delaney's daughter Laura, and their boy, the half-brother he had never seen, was that what she meant by his "people"? Or was it Aunt Jo and Jimmy, just turned eleven, down in Macleod? Not Uncle Pat, dead now for six years.

"I'm an orphan, ma'am." He saw the look of dismay on her face, and almost felt sorry for her. She hadn't been snooping. But people just didn't know how some questions came like scraping a wound with a rough board, the sharp pain pulsing in like lightning, pulsing throbs. It echoed the pain he'd felt ten years back, two months after his mother's death (had he called her Ma, Mom, what, he couldn't remember?), when he was just starting to feel like a normal seven-year-old boy again, and his father sat him down for a talk.

He was marrying Grace, his father said. Man was not meant to live alone. Grace was a wonderful woman and would bring up Laura well. But not him, Burt, and the baby, Jimmy. Grace didn't feel right about bringing up boys, a whole family. Laura, at four, would be able to adjust. Burton, you're a fine young strong man, and you will grow to understand. Your Aunt Jo and Uncle Pat— she's my sister over in Montana—why they would be happy to have two boys to raise.

The next two weeks had passed in one long soundless scream of pain, until Mr. and Mrs. Pat Garrity arrived, spent two days, and departed on the Great Northern with a seven year old, and a baby just turned one.

The woman hadn't recovered her composure. Burt was still staring at her, and he saw her flit a glance to her husband, who was helping his eight year old daughter with her meat cutting. The mother flushed and said, "Oh, I'm so terribly sorry. I shouldn't have... Was it, was it recently?"

"No ma'am, ten years, about." Ten years since his father had died to him. Maybe he should have said six, to honour Pat Garrity, the old Irish soldier who had been much more a real father. "It's all right, really, I got used to it."

To be used to something didn't mean understanding it. He turned to his plate again, not hungry, but hoping she was. He chewed methodically, swallowed one bite and got the next one in. She gazed at him for a few seconds, and picked up her knife and fork. There was silence at their end of the table. Burt saw her husband look at her, seeing the red flush in her cheeks, and forming a silent question with his mouth. She shook her head slightly, and the husband turned again to the little girl.

Their name was Jackson. He worked for Breckenridge and Lund, the construction company from Fernie that was going to build the new spur line. Why had he brought his whole family to Frank? Maybe it was a holiday, and she and the children would be going home soon, while he stayed for the job, which would probably take two or three months. That was a family for you. He looked over her head at the boy sitting opposite his sister. The father smiled at the boy and there was an answering flash of joy. That man would never just cut his family in half.

Up in his room again, he saw that he'd left the lamp on, and muttered in annoyance. It wasn't the coal oil, that was cheap, it was the danger. The wood in this boarding house had been up almost two years, and it was seasoned now, all the boards shrunk and letting in the breeze that constantly swept down the pass. One stupid mistake and two dozen people could die a horrible death. He'd seen it happen, been in two fires. The second one claimed Pat Garrity.

It was completely dark now, and he shrugged himself into his pea jacket. It would be getting cold. Normally, he caught another two hours of sleep after dinner, but now he absolutely had to get out of the house. Once past the front door, he paused between the two big pines. At the supper table, that had been the first time it had struck him in over a month, that shot of pain. And all because he didn't chew fast enough to stop her from talking! He turned up the collar of the jacket, pushing his shoulders up, making himself invulnerable again, He turned left and stepped onto the continuation of Dominion Avenue, though it certainly didn't look like a road here. To the CPR tracks, then back, would be about a mile walk.

After two hundred yards, he hit the end of the sidewalk. It was duckboards in ten foot lengths, scraps of lumber nailed to two thin tops of lodgepole pine. There had been a thaw two weeks ago, and the mud had frozen unevenly, so that each length of sidewalk was an adventure. Stepping on one end would raise the other end in the air, often a foot or more. A teeter-totter, but one with the additional hazard of missing bits of board. You watched where you stepped, or you turned an ankle. Burt found the footing better inside the mine.

Light flooded out of the Palm Restaurant. The owner had gone overboard on the lights when the electric power station started up, buying twenty drop lights for his business. Back at the boarding house, electric lights were limited to the main floor and not all of it. Burt was just in front of the restaurant when the sidewalk rose six inches under him, throwing him off stride.

It was Corporal Allen, coming along behind him. He or Constable Leard could be counted on to patrol the downtown and out into the flats east of Gold Creek at least twice a night. "Who's that?" boomed the corporal's voice, and Burt pulled down the collar of his jacket. "Oh, it's you, young fellow. Delaney, isn't it?"

"Yes, sir." Burt was impressed with both of the Northwest Mounted Police officers. They accepted "Sirs", quite naturally, they never raised their voices beyond a parade ground pitch, they could walk through a melee of brawling miners without ever getting a smudge on a uniform, and they treated their horses right. It was funny: the NWMP and the Indians were the only people he'd seen out here who treated horses with real affection, the police grooming them meticulously and the Indians not at all, but both groups constantly petting, touching, talking to their mounts.

"Out for a stroll?" Corporal Allen would probably pass a word with fifty men on his own stroll through town tonight. He knew the town. Burt wondered if anyone ever called Corporal Allen "Jack", which was, many swore, his given name. He doubted it. Last summer, when Burt first came to Frank, both officers had casually interrogated him, found out where he came from, what he wanted to do. He had been angry at first, and then he saw that it was universal. Now he just nodded, and the two walked side by side. The Mountie would be turning in to the Imperial Hotel, just showing his face for a minute to the bartender as a reminder that too much drink sold might be reason for less leniency if the hotel were to be caught in any infraction. The system worked.

The CPR station was a boxcar fitted with a peaked roof. It was dark and silent. Burt turned and went back on the west side of Dominion. Now he could sleep till about eleven. The night foreman would be meeting the whole shift just before midnight. Fourteen months, twenty-five or twenty-six shifts a month, this was something he could get through. He could get through anything.

Chapter 2

Laura Freeman checked off another day on the shop calendar. April 24th, there you go, even though it's only ten in the morning, I can still say that April 24th has come and has been met. Five more days and I can go home. No more Sanatorium, no more of that foul smelling hot water, home to the clean brightness of the ranch. What was she homesick for most? She had a list memorized, counted out on her fingers hundreds of times while soaking in the hot baths at the San. Mum and Da, of course. Mum's cooking. Ginger—she doubted that anyone gave her half the rides she needed to keep in shape. Holly Kerwin, with her sense of humour and her wildness. And seeing the sun come up out of flatness. Mountains in the west, where they belonged, not all around you like here. Buffalo beans in bloom, but that would be summer. The open prairie around Pincher Creek.

What would she miss, leaving Frank? Gerry, maybe the nicest older brother in the world. Florence Warrington had turned into a good friend, but she was leaving Frank too, probably three days after Laura. Laura wondered how serious Florence was about Alex Dixon, who had been visiting the Warringtons, and was going to accompany Florence to Ontario. Alex looked like a suitor, and who would come thousands of miles just to do a favour for a former neighbour? Yes, she'd miss Florence, but she had an idea that she'd be writing to her next year as Mrs. Dixon.

Gerry was having his tea in the kitchen. He'd gotten to work in the front room shop about seven this morning to finish some half soles he'd promised for the afternoon. They were on the counter, and Laura picked up the first pair, brown brogues. She slipped on some rough gloves and began to apply a little polish, working it in with a bit of water from a bowl. There! Now let them dry while I put some blacking on the other pair. Five minutes brushing and they'll look like they were just bought in London, England!

The little forest of lasts, a whole dance troupe upside down, was sadly out of order. Gerry always put the last last, the final last, the end-of-work last, down at the end of the row, regardless of its size, and half his work day seemed to be occupied with searching for a "LEFT SEVEN DAMMIT". That was the only time he ever swore, and she couldn't get him to stop. Nor could she ever get him to put lasts in their proper order. Now she sorted them out, knowing that in a few days, disorder would reign again.

The bell was tipped by the opening door just as she straightened up from her sorting job. It was that young man who had dropped in at the Warringtons' house last Christmas, while she was visiting Florence. He worked the night shift with Florence's father, she knew that. She started off, hoping the name would just pop into her head. "Hello! You're Mr. ..." and of course it failed.

"Delaney," he supplied, and then grinned. "And you are Miss Freeman."

"That's not fair. You knew where you were coming, and I had no chance to think."

"There's also the fact that there's a lot more dirty-faced fellows around here than there are young ladies." True, there were some lines of coal graven into his face, but he was as clean as any miner could reasonably be. She smiled back. If he was flirting, it was harmless. Florence had said her father thought Mr. Delaney to be a good worker, not experienced, but very good with the mine horses, and willing to put his back into it when required.

"I believe you have some work boots here for me. They're older ones that I bought from Shorty... uh, Mr. Dawson, and your brother was fixing them up for me. They're black." They both laughed. Whatever colour boots were when they went into that mine, they became black and stayed black.

Laura turned to the shelves behind the counter, checking the tags tied to eyelets. "Here they are. New soles, new nails, new heels, new plates, stretched. Keep the trees in them when you're not wearing them, for at least a month. All the time is even better. That will be one dollar, seventy-five."

He produced two American silver dollars. That was how the mine paid. She looked for coins, but the drawer was practically empty. "Can you take a shinplaster?"

"Oh, yes. I use them at the restaurant."

"Aren't you at the boarding house? I thought Lillian Clark said that you ..."

She couldn't go on with the rest of Lillian Clark's admiring comments about young Mr. Delaney. "Burton," Lillian had said, "but Da says they call him Burt, like Bert, but with a "u". He's ever so handsome!"

"I am. But when I went on night shift, I changed to just supper and the lunch pail. When I want something during the day, if I'm awake, I'll get it at the Palm. Mr. Bell has me take care of his horse sometimes, and I get a credit there. But a shinplaster will come in handy for an extra."

He was interesting. Most young miners were half drunk for three days after payday, and stony broke till the next. "Excuse my curiosity, Mr. Delaney, but where are you from?" Everyone in Frank over the age of two was from somewhere else. Some of the six hundred residents had been in that curious crowd that came for the 'grand opening' of the town in September, 1901. Gerry had come to that ceremony, and had moved his shop up here a month later, though he had chosen the flats here east of town where the land was free for the squatting, while a business lot in town cost about five hundred dollars.

"Oh, lots of places. Minneapolis first, I guess, then Great Falls, then a lot of ranches,, finally Macleod. Now Frank, but not forever Frank."

"Nor I! Next week it's back home to Pincher Creek for me. Now, that's not glamorous like Great Falls or Minnea ... whatever you said, but it's home and I'm going!" Suddenly she was ashamed of her glee. "I don't mean that Frank's not a nice place in some ways, but..."

"It's not home, that's for sure. But it's beautiful here this morning. I saw a crocus on the way over here."

"You did! I haven't been out of the house at all this morning, and there's a crocus out there! You'll have to show me. Gerry!" Her call was answered by a crash from the kitchen. "Wait here, Mr. Delaney, I'll be back in a flash."

Gerry was standing staring down at the remains of a saucer on the wooden floor of the kitchen. "Those things aren't much use, are they, Laura? I mean, you move your mug the least bit near the end of the table, and the next thing, well, they're gone, never having done a useful thing in their whole existence. D'ye think maybe we should just glue them to the table?"

It didn't matter. She was already sweeping the fragments into a dustpan. "Gerry, Mr. Delaney, you know, the young man, he's picked up the boots, and now he's going to show me where he saw a crocus on the way over. It's spring!"

A minute later she had a shawl on and was out the door. Burton Delaney was waiting on the path. The sun actually felt hot on her face. One small tennis ball of cloud was poised above the summit of Turtle Mountain, and the whole arch of the sky was a bright blue. A few lines of trees showed on a sloping bench half way down the mountain. Then there was the dull brown of the cheat grass down the slope to the trees along the Oldman River, mostly evergreen but with a splash of yellowy green where willows were bursting out. She could hear the rush of water in Gold Creek a few hundred yards to her right. The Oldman might be in flood too, but they were high enough here. Anyway, the slope to the east was enough to keep the river turbulently on its way down to the prairies.

"Here's one." Burton Delaney was pointing to a little purple flower a few yards off to the right of the path, the north side, towards the CPR tracks. "Not even the one I saw on the way over." and then there was another, and another. They were over to the embankment now, where the south slope had been snow free for over a week.

Before they knew it, they were looking at the back yard of Jack Dawes' log cabin. Jack and his two Welsh friends were working day shift, so the two young people didn't worry as they cut through beside the cabin to come out to the path again just past the livery stable.

"Hello, Burt." That was Frank Rochette, the stableman. "Walking young Laura about now, are yeh?" Burt Delaney actually looked flustered, and Laura almost giggled.

"Enough of your teasing, Mr. Rochette. Mr. Delaney was just showing me some crocuses. Did you know they were out?"

"Sure, but what difference? Here in the pass we can get a big blow any day, and then they'll just have to come another week, won't they?" Frank was short and dark, with a square face and black eyes. Robert Watt, the stable boss, said that Frank was a "might be" meaning a Métis who wasn't admitting anything. Frank usually just grinned and said he'd wait to see how the next fight was going.

Laura had never seen Frank without that wide flashing grin. It was usually he who brought the horses over to the mine entrance, trailing them along the east bank of Gold Creek and coaxing them along the planks of the bridge over the Oldman. Florence had said that it was Burt who often did the return trip, bringing horses who stabled overnight at the mine.

There were two horses around the side of the stable where a lean-to covered some hay. Frank was bringing out a third, a big bay cross. "That's Charley, isn't he?" Burt asked, moving toward the horse. Laura followed him, but a few steps back. She knew it was a rare horse that liked more than two people up close.

"Yeah, just coming up on the end of his holidays. Needed shoeing, and I think he needed sun just as much. Back to the pit tomorrow, old boy." Frank patted Charley's withers, and Burt did the same. "Don't you worry, Miss Laura, he don't bite."

"I know." She felt annoyed. "Don't be forgetting I've handled a few horses."

"Nothing meant, for sure. How's the rheumatiz? Them baths up there work?"

"Yes they do. They're boring and they stink, but I'm sure moving a lot better. Going home in five days."

"That'll be nice for you. Nothing like home." She felt a twinge of pity for him. No home, no family, just the horses. Looking at Burt Delaney on the far side of the horse, she wondered where his family was. He'd said Minneapolis, then Great Falls, then Macleod, but that's all he said. Just that Frank was not home, nor would it be his home. But he didn't have the air of a drifter. He looked like he had a schedule.

So did Charley. The other two horses were busy at the hay, and he wanted his share. He snorted and jerked his head up. Frank laughed and turned him towards the side of the stable. Burt and Laura were left on the path.

"Well, then. Enough crocuses?"

She smiled. "We've seen more than you promised. And I guess you want to get those boots home to make sure they fit. They may seem tight for a few days, but work them in."

He looked down at the boots as if he'd forgotten them. "Oh, yes. Thanks very much. Would you like to help me use up that shin-plaster at the Palm?"

Was he being cheeky? Maybe this is what went on in Macleod, down on the plains, but in Pincher Creek, a stranger didn't just ask a girl to go to a restaurant just like that! Not that she'd ever met a stranger in Pincher Creek, one her age. She'd known everybody forever there. Maybe ... but Gerry would worry. "No, thank you very much, Mr. Delaney, but I can't...today." Why had she paused there? He might think she wanted to... oh, no, he couldn't, he knew she was leaving in just five days.

"Maybe sometime before you leave, then. I've really enjoyed meeting you... I mean, really meeting you, not like Christmas."

"And I've enjoyed talking with you. Yes, maybe before I leave."

"I'm on steady nights, so any evening is fine."

"But you already pay for supper at the boarding house, you said."

"It still wouldn't be bad to miss one." He grinned. "But maybe after service on Sunday? You and your brother. And maybe then we can call each other Burt and Laura. Old American custom. Irish too, I think."

"Oh, I think we can manage that right now, Burt. Now I'd better be heading back, or Gerry will worry. I'll leave a message at the boarding house about Sunday. No, don't bother to walk me back, you've got a shift tonight, haven't you? And no sleep yet today, I'll bet."

"You're right there. And supper to deal with. Fish tonight, and I hope it's fresher than last week's. Goodbye, Laura, and thank you again for your company. It's been like ... well, like the first crocus in Frank."

When she reached the door of Gerry's shop, she turned. He was out of sight where the trail curved alongside the creek, but she could see the far end of the bridge. After half a minute, she saw him there. To her surprise, he turned and waved. She waved back, and went into the shop.

Chapter 3

The Palm Restaurant would soon go out of business in Macleod, Burt thought as he waited at the second table. Mrs. Bell had offered to bring him coffee, but he preferred to wait for Laura and her brother to get out of the Presbyterian service down the street and join him. Lillian Clark had brought him the message yesterday, just as he'd been wondering if his invitation had been too quick, too breezy. Particularly him saying "after service" like that. A few months ago, he'd seen them emerge from the little white church, and so he'd known which service they attended, but maybe the words had given her the idea that he was Presbyterian too, just a non-attender.

Sometimes, once a month or so, he went over to Blairmore for mass. Uncle Pat had been Irish Catholic, but he had also been Army. He was unswervable in religion, but a bit inattentive, and his years of wrangling in the Plains hadn't made him a bit pious. Aunt Jo was the same, though she did keep Burt and Jimmy at their prayers. He could barely remember how his mother felt or acted about church, though he had a vivid picture of kneeling beside her in the big cathedral in Minneapolis, his father on her other side, Laura completing the family pew. His mother had usually worn a dark green velvet gown to church, with a broad fashionable hat. What had he worn? He remembered a tight jacket of rough wool tweed, short pants, but tight, to just below the knee, then stockings and leather shoes—the only time in the week he wore shoes in warm weather, He'd been about to start altar boy training when she died and his world ended.

In Montana, there was family again. Only now, if and when they got to a church, he was always sitting beside Pat, while Jimmy was in Aunt Jo's arms or on her lap. No question of altar boy training, and little chance of seeing the same priest two years in a row. Pat sometimes grumbled that he, a blasphemous sergeant of the Inniskillings, knew more Latin than some of these prairie priests.

"Why did you come to America, Uncle Pat?"

"Restlessness, Burty, just restlessness. There's me squadron commander off to Ottawa on Staff to his Excellency, and I begs him to take me along as groom. Never ran a stable under twelve good mounts, did Captain Aikenhead, and I soon had him convinced that them Canadians didn't know a horse from a donkey. Some of them didn't, too. Well, he got me seconded and out I came, 1880. Then, five years later, he's getting ready to go back home... no, not home, but over to England to the real Staff. Just then Riel kicks over the traces in the Territories, and I sees my chance. The captain gave me his blessing and I wangled a job as groom for Sir William Otter, and within a week, I was on a train for Qu'Appelle on the Saskatchewan."

"Gosh, was that like Custer and the Last Stand?"

"Lordy, no! This was organized British Army fashion, sonny. Damned few regulars, mostly Ontario militia, but good lads, willing, if a little raw. Otter marched our column, near six hundred of us, up to Battleford pretty sharply. No cavalry to speak of, infantry, and two little dinky seven pounders. A Cree chief named Poundmaker was maybe hooking up with Riel, him and Big Bear, who'd been burning and looting near Battleford. Well, after sitting in town for a bit, Otter decided to prod Poundmaker, and about half our force marched out to his camp by Cut Knife Creek. Like kicking an ant heap it was, you do it because you're curious, then you wish you hadn't got what you found. Those Indians were all over us! Pretty soon we were almost surrounded, and we had to just fire, load, fire for hours, so much smoke you couldn't aim hardly. One Gatling Gun, operated by an American who was trying to sell them to the Dominion Government, but it didn't do much good that I could see. Otter was pretty cool headed, I'll say that. He got the force out with a fighting withdrawal, short bounds. Eight men killed, thirteen wounded, and we got them all out except for one poor lad whose body had rolled into a coulee."

"A lot luckier than Custer, right?"

"A lot smarter than Custer is more like it. Not that the prodding was too smart, but at least Otter didn't go hell for leather into a fight with no support. And Poundmaker was getting a little nervous over the whole thing anyway. Riel surrendered after Battleford and Fish Creek, and then Poundmaker came in and surrendered. Then we spent one of the stupidest months of my life, about six hundred of us looking for Big Bear, who was damned near alone. We finally got back to Battleford on the first of July, and then Big Bear surrenders to the Northwest Mounted Police way over at Fort Carlton. And that was that, pretty small praties, right? But, y'know, it settled that the Territories was Canadian, not whatever Riel might have made it. Poor devil was half nuts, and he had a lot of right on his side, I'll admit. No Irishman would ever say that dealing with the English is easy. But compared with what went on over the line in the States, I figure that the Métis and the two bands of Cree that rebelled got off light.

"Anyway, I really liked the West, even after that June of skeeters and hail and what-not, combing both sides of the North Saskatchewan for one very sneaky Indian. I decided to take my discharge out there. Hooked up with some cattle drivers who'd brought meat up from the Dakotas to supply the North West Field Force, and set up for a cowboy. Mainly as an ostler, farrier, we'd call it back home. So across the line I went, and a year later I go for a toot in Minneapolis, and there I met Jo. The year you were born, 1886. We were at your christening, though you wouldn't remember. She went back to Montana with me, and we ranched for a bit, but I could do better working the stables of the big ranches, and Jo—well, you know—is one of the world's great cooks. Then your mum died, and we got you and Jimmy, and never been sorry a minute about that!"

"What was my mum like, Uncle Pat?"

"Well, I've told you a few times, and I'll tell you again. She was a lot like Jo, but quieter. Your da, I never knew too good, but I know he writes to you. Don't get down, Burty, it don't help to think about some things. Come on, I'll show you something with that rope."

"Dreaming?"

This time, the voice was not in his head, but out there, and he looked up. Laura was there, with her brother Gerry, the shoemaker, behind her. For a few seconds, Burt swung back and forth between the worlds of 1897 Montana and 1903 Frank. That had been in the late summer of 1897, a month before Pat Garrity's sudden death in a barn fire, Now the heat and the dust of that ranch north of Great Falls seemed as immediate and real as the spring sunshine on the mud of Dominion Street outside the Palm Restaurant. Then he shook himself and rose. "Sorry, I guess I was. Dreaming, I mean. I was thinking about my uncle. Down in Montana."

"Oh, yes, you said you'd lived in Great Falls. Is it all right for us to sit?" She was grinning at him, and he felt even more flustered. He almost knocked one chair over getting it from the table. Suddenly he wondered what Gerry must be thinking about him. Mrs. Bell saved him by appearing beside the table just as Laura was settling in her chair.

"Would you be wanting coffee and maybe some scones, Burt?" Jessie Bell was a large woman with a beaming round face, a face Burt had never seen with a cross line in it.

"Yes, thank you very much, Mrs. Bell. Unless … is coffee… um …acceptable?" Laura's grin widened, but she nodded, and so did Gerry.

"Were you a ranch hand down there? I noticed you handle horses easily."

"No. Well, in a way. But we left Montana in '98, after my uncle died. He was the man for horses. I think he talked to them in Irish, and they liked that. But I was still pretty small, and ranching was going different, range closing, and sheep taking over in parts. It was more open up here in the Territory, and my aunt decided to come over the line. Then she got a boarding house in Macleod, and that's where I was till last June when I came out here."

Laura leaned forward on her elbows. He was acutely aware of Gerry sitting beside him, leaning back, smiling. Laura said, "See Gerry, I'm finding out everything about the mysterious Mr. Delaney. Why, we asked Lillian Clark where you came from, and even she didn't know. So now, I'm feeling like one of those detectives. So, on to the next question, like that Sherlock Holmes you're always reading about. Mr. Delaney, can you explain to us exactly why a healthy young man would leave perfectly good ranch country and work in a coal pit?"

"Not forever. I think I said that to you the other day."

"Yes, you did. And I, for one, think you very wise. A mine forever would be a black future, wouldn't it? But what future are you thinking of?"

He realized that she would never be talking like this without her brother present, and he turned to Gerry. "Do you have to explain to her every morning why you do what you do?"

"No," Gerry drawled. "But she's not as curious about me as she is about you. The last two days have been Mr. Delaney this and Mr. Delaney that. Perhaps you should write out your life history so she can take it back to Pincher Creek and memorize it."

Laura had turned very pink even to the edge of red. "That's nonsense, Gerry. A couple of questions, after all, are reasonable if you're going to go out for coffee with a young miner, even a reluctant miner. And I have *lots* of things to do in Pincher Creek."

It was good to see that she got flustered too. Burt smiled at her, and she smiled back. "No, not a miner forever." he said. "I'm saving up. There's some really interesting country west of here, over in Columbia, British Columbia. Dry ranch country, but lots of river water, creeks coming down from the hills, never dries up. I figure if I can save up some money I can go out there next year and start my own ranch. Small, maybe a thousand head." That was enough to say. No need to go into the problem of getting Aunt Jo and Jimmy out there too.

"But you said you had an aunt? Is she going to stay in Macleod?"

"For a year or so. Her and Jimmy…" He stopped. She knew nothing of Jimmy, or Aunt Jo for that matter, and he couldn't think of any reason she should know. Then he realized that just leaving the name hanging over the table wouldn't work either. "Jimmy, that's my brother. He's eleven now. If I can get a ranch going, well, that'll be two years anyway, they might move out then. Jimmy likes the open air."

"So do you, I know. But you're working in that mine. That's awful."

"It's not that bad. A bit nervy sometimes, all the creaking of the pit timbers and everything. Sometimes you think you're in the stomach of something huge, and it's moving around trying to digest you or hold you away from the world."

"They call it 'Walking Mountain.'" This was Gerry, the first words he'd addressed directly to Burt.

"Who?"

"Peigans. Probably the tribes west of the pass, too. You knew they never camped here?"

Burt knew something along that line, but he couldn't think what. "Well, who knows why an Indian camps?"

"Same reason we all do, to sleep. But not by Turtle Mountain." The shoemaker leaned back again. "Maybe it's the shape. Or the Oldman River. Peigans love that water, all the way down to where it slows down and gets muddy. Anyway, they don't camp in this part of the pass."

Laura was fussing with her hat, drawing out a pin about six inches long. Burt switched his attention to her and said, "You're taking the train back to Pincher Creek, Miss Freeman?"

Her annoyance was real. "We said it would be Burt and Laura, remember? Well, I'm *Laura*, Mister Delaney. Yes. The early morning train on Wednesday."

"I'm sorry. You're looking forward to getting home, I expect. Are you right in town?"

"No, we're about four miles north. Gerry used to walk in to open his store. Here he sleeps in till all hours. But not next weekend, after he loses the best helper he ever had."

"A moderately good helper, when she stays in the shop and doesn't wander all over town delivering notes." Gerry moved back to let Jessie Bell put down a plate of scones.

"Well it will be interesting to see how you find your lasts next week. You just watch, Burt, you'll be seeing people limping because they have a nine on one foot and a five on the other, both pointing left."

There was no embarrassment in her face now, Burt thought. Her eyes were a light green, her lashes almost invisible, but her eyebrows positive, almost bushy. Her hair was hidden by the wide hat, but he remembered from the crocus-hunting day that it was brown, actually tan, thick and straight. Was she sixteen or seventeen? Probably sixteen, he thought. He wondered what she read. Suddenly her mouth turned down and he realized he'd been staring.

"I'm sorry. I was just wondering ..."

"What?"

"What do you read?"

Gerry choked on the scone he was eating, spraying crumbs across the table. For a moment Burt and Laura stared at him, then grinned at each other. The coughing died down, Gerry leaned back and pounded his chest with both hands. "Read? Read? Why, anything with words. All the time. I've even seen her on her horse, reading away. Maybe to the horse, I wasn't close enough to tell." He was breathing more easily now. "Burt, if you have books, prepare to lose them now."

Laura joined in, "Friends, fellow citizens of Frank, lend me your volumes."

"Mine is the barest bookcase of them all." Burt knew some Shakespeare, but not from reading. Pat Garrity would recite for hours. "Miners travel light. But later, I'm going to read everything I can."

"What is it like there, in the mountain?" Laura looked serious now.

"Not so terrible as you might think. It is dirty, of course, because the coal dust just hangs in the air, even on the night shift, when we're not taking coal out, just working on the pipes and timbers. But we have good ventilation—that's what the other men tell me, though this is the first mine I've worked in myself. We're about five thousand feet in, going on an upward angle to follow the seam. Good working space, about twelve or thirteen feet wide, and you can stand up straight most of the time. And our adit goes up, so we have the fall working for us, and really the horses have their toughest job pulling the empty wagons up to the face. Coming down, they just lean back, keeping the wagon from running down the adit. Oh, I don't like it compared with working outside with good animals. But it's not that bad. There are some strong people who have been digging in the muck for years."

Laura looked puzzled. "What does that mean, the 'adit'?"

"Oh, that's the hole you see in the mountain. When the hole goes down, it's a shaft. When it goes straight in, it's an adit. The interesting thing about Turtle Mountain is that nobody had to prospect it. The coal seam sits out there saying 'Follow me'. And it's almost straight up and down. We can't take everything out, but the way the seam is, it's not hard to get a lot of tonnage out to the tip. But my job now is maintaining, fixing timbers, working on the track. It's the men on the day shift who move the coal."

"It still must be frightening, inside that mountain all night, in the dark."

"It is good to come out in the morning and see the sun slanting up the valley. Some mornings we could probably see the shadow of your house in Pincher Creek, the sun's so low. Big house? Got a barn?"

"Both. And some nice horses. Do you ride, Burt? Maybe, after I get home, I could ask my parents if you could come down for a few days. What do you think, Gerry?"

"Oh, I'm sure they'd like to meet your young man, little sister."

That suggestion silenced the enthusiasts. Both got very busy with the rest of the scones and the coffee.

Chapter 4

Laura leaned back into the big wing chair and looked over the hotel lobby with satisfaction. The Frank Hotel wasn't as big as the Imperial, but Gerry had chosen it because he knew the owner, Mr. Manual, and probably because he thought its public bar would be quieter. She hoped it wouldn't be totally silent; after all, she had to have some stories to take back to Pincher Creek tomorrow.

Across from her, a man was dozing on the chesterfield, not a miner, for he didn't have those striped lines of black in the folds of the skin. Maybe someone from the CPR, though his suit was grey, not navy blue. His breath moved his moustaches in a steady rhythm, the hairs on each side of his mouth flaring out, then falling back untidily. Past his right shoulder was the hotel desk, with young George Somebody behind it. He'd had some shoes repaired in March, and had tried to impress her with talk of Calgary. As if that were a place one would want to call home!

Her bag was up in their room, and Gerry had wanted to leave her there as well. After checking in, he'd realized that the gift belt for their father was back in the shop. It was important that Laura be the bearer of the gift, since she would be sure to tell Da how many hours had been spent tooling the design, and how tricky the hammering of the buckle had been. He would just dash back to the shop, he said, and she could wait in the room.

"Nonsense!" was the immediate reaction. "I can sit perfectly safely in the lobby, Gerry, under the eye of Mr. Manual. When you said we'd spend the last night in town, it was so we could have some fun, an adventure, wasn't it? It's not too adventurous sitting in a stuffy room while you walk all the way to the shop and back."

He had given in. He always did when she really meant her protests. So now she was there in the lobby, almost evening, with people passing back and forth, miners peering out from the bar door, then disappearing behind it, some songs emerging when the door was open, not terribly loud but … would the word be 'raucous'? Maybe, but also fun. She thought about the men in there, big men who had spent their day out of the spring sunlight. Some of them would be getting out the cards, ready to bet a week's wages for excitement, for a change from the everlasting view of a coal face.

How did Burt Delaney feel about that, the mine, the monotony? She didn't know him at all well enough, but she liked him. When they'd sat in the Palm Restaurant on Sunday, she'd felt that he was caught between lives, as she was. She was, or thought she was, someone who would always want to be on a ranch, not a big one, but a place where you could ride in one direction for half an hour and not set hoof on a neighbour's property. Well, maybe not quite half an hour, twenty minutes would do. But Burt had described a dark place where you had to turn sideways to get through between coal and rock. A place where six more feet of coal seam meant more to the owners than a square mile of the surface might mean to her father. Now she had been caught in Frank for a winter, in the Sanatorium, and she'd felt hemmed in. Tomorrow morning, early, she would catch the train east to home and freedom. And at the time she was leaving, the night shift would be coming out of the mine, blinking in the sun reflected from Crowsnest Mountain. Burt had said that next year he would be leaving.

She pushed back in the big wing chair and looked at the big wooden fan slowly revolving and swirling the smoke in the lobby.

It was silly. There were a hundred miners here in Frank, and she had met Burt Delaney three times. Tomorrow, she'd be back home. Her father would be at the Pincher Creek station with the cart (though she wished he'd bring Ginger, but her suitcase needed the cart. Maybe he'd bring the cart <u>and</u> Ginger?) No more Burt Delaney, and what would that matter? She frowned at the fan. It just wasn't right to start to like someone, and then decide it made no matter.

Gerry liked him too. Maybe Gerry and Burt would become friends, maybe Gerry would insist on bringing Burt down to Pincher Creek for a visit. That would be good. She could picture him running his hand over Ginger's withers. Ginger would be startled at first, dance aside, but Laura knew that Burt wouldn't be bothered by that, that his hand would follow, not too quickly, but steadily, and Ginger would find it soothing. It was a good picture. She could see the afternoon sun slanting down from the Rockies, the shadow of the man and the mare extending for a hundred yards, the grey lodgepole pine fence behind them.

"Must be thinking of something nice." It was Burt Delaney. How long had he been there?

"Why Mr. Delaney, you startled me…"

"It's Burt, Laura. I thought we'd settled that. Twice. I saw Gerry heading back to the house, and he said you were here, that the two of you were having a go away party in town."

"Yes, it's such an early train, and such a nice night, and Gerry thought … well, he thought it would be relaxing to be here and all packed. Are you working tonight?" Of course he was, he was steady nights, six days a week.

"I am, but I had a good sleep today, so I'm just going to wander around until I have to change and go to work. In fact, I was just turning down towards your place when I met Gerry. I was going to say goodbye, and ask you to do me a favour."

"Of course. I should say, what favour, I may not be able to... but if I can, why, certainly, whatever it is. The favour, I mean." She was having trouble with her tongue for some reason.

He was wearing a woollen jacket, the type they called Norfolk, and he reached into an inside pocket. "I was taking these to the station to be franked, but the agent isn't there. The regular man. The fellow at the window didn't know how to do the franking." He withdrew two long white envelopes from the jacket. "Could you have it done at Pincher Creek? I've got the amount marked on each, the amount it should be. It adds up to a dollar ten, so I could give you a dollar and a shinplaster, would that be right?"

"Of course. I'll even make my fee, won't I?" She smiled to make the joke clear, for he looked terribly serious. "Where are they going?"

"One just down to Macleod, to my aunt. The other is to Minnesota. That's the one that will cost the most." He handed the envelopes to her. The one on top was addressed to Mr. James Delaney, General Delivery in Minneapolis. Burt had said something about living in Minneapolis once, but he'd also said something about his parents being dead. Maybe this was an uncle. She wasn't going to ask. Two days before, talking in the restaurant, she had said something about her mother and father, and pain had run across his face like a ripple in water.

She stood up suddenly. "Heavens, here I am gawking up at you, my neck will be sore. Isn't there somewhere you can sit?" He glanced at the chesterfield, and she saw that the man in the gray suit had gone over to the desk and was talking with Mr. Manual. Burt and Laura crossed to the chesterfield and sat.

"You must be looking forward to getting home."

His tone was so flat. She turned to him and saw that he was looking straight ahead. "Yes, I am. You've been through Pincher Creek, haven't you?"

"Only on the train, and at night. But I think I know what it's like. High prairie, no trees, lots of sky and plenty of coulees, am I right?"

"Yes, but also sun like you never get here. Down home, the mountains shine, they don't block the sun—they're the bright edge on the west. And you can ride." She'd told him about Ginger two days before, and seen his interest. "You love horses, don't you, Burt?"

"Yes. I want to have a lot of them, and I will. Not here, not in the territories. But a man was telling me there's a place west of here, halfway through British Columbia, where there's hardly any people homesteading yet. Dry, but lots of creeks coming down from the mountains, so your stock can always water, and you just need some bottom land for hay. That's where I'm aiming for. But I told you all this on Sunday, didn't I?"

"You said halfway through. If I were to look on a map, what would I look for?"

"The main thing is a long lake called Okanagan. Keegan, one of the men at the mine, comes from Trail, and two years ago he went west to that valley. He says in the north there's good cattle country, and there's some big ranches in the south end, down by the border with the States. It gets a lot drier south of the border. I've gotten used to Canada, and Jimmy—well, he'd hardly remember Montana."

"Or Minn-e-ap-olis," she offered, reading it from the envelope." I wonder if he'll explain, she thought, and then worried when a grim look crossed his face, "I'm sorry. It's none of my business."

"No, its all right. I've got you sending my letters for me, and anyway ... I don't really like to talk about this, but you deserve an explanation, I mean it's not your fault that I get all ... upset, I guess."

"You don't really have to explain anything to me, Burt. I mean, I really like you, it's been fun knowing you, but tomorrow ... you know."

He smiled. "You go away, and maybe we'll never see each other again, and that's not going to make me happy. I had a plan all worked out, Laura. I was going to wait a week or so, then ask Gerry for your mailing address. Then I was going to write to you, just tell you what was happening in Frank, what the weather was like and everything, and I was going to just hope that you'd answer, and we could write a lot. Then maybe we could meet again. But it wouldn't work out if I'm always acting the man of mystery, would it? So here goes."

He touched the envelope in her hand. "That's addressed to my father. I said I was an orphan, I know, because, in a way, he made me one. When my mother died, I was seven. Suddenly, he wanted to get married again, and the woman—her name was Grace—she didn't want boys. She was willing to keep my little sister, like she was a doll or something, but me, I was too noisy, too dirty, too much a boy, she said. And Jimmy, the baby, why he'd grow into a boy too, so he couldn't stay with them. My father just went along with her ideas as if he didn't have any will of his own, and Jimmy and I got farmed out to Aunt Jo and Uncle Pat." He touched the other envelope. "She's been wonderful to me, and I love her a lot. But I still get mad."

"That's awful, Burt. To do something like that. Jimmy, well I guess he'd be too young for it to bother him, but at seven it must have been terrible for you." She felt a wave of warmth go through her body, an urge to just hug him and comfort him. Then it turned into a blush.

"You're the first person I've ever told since I was twelve or so. Before that, I used to tell all sorts of people, and it looked like I wanted their pity or something, so I stopped. I had to learn to be strong and make my own life work, get my own ranch, take care of Aunt Jo and Jimmy, and not keep crying about the past."

"But it keeps coming back, I guess." She held up the Minneapolis letter.

"He wrote to me. He wants me to visit there. Says Grace is different somehow, and I should go over to see them. And tell him all is forgiven, I suppose."

"Are you going to?"

"Maybe when it rains potatoes." His tone was bitter. "No, I told him—there," and he tapped the envelope, "that giving up people is something that you do for keeps, because Jimmy and I don't need him or his Grace, and he should just leave us alone." His mouth tightened, his lips almost white with compression. "The hard part is that I wish I could see my sister. Her name is Laura, too, did I mention that?"

She shook her head. She felt a stinging at the back of her eyes, and prayed that she wouldn't cry. Pity would drive him away.

"She'd be fourteen now. She had black, black hair and eyes, and very pale skin. I wish she'd been a tomboy, and then we could have stayed together. Grace wouldn't have wanted her. But no, she was very quiet and sweet. Maybe some day, we'll get to meet, if I can work out a way to do it without..."

"Without seeing your father."

"That's right."

A whole jumble of advice swirled through her mind. Forgive that ye may be forgiven. Hate corrodes the soul. Everyone deserves a second chance. Saying any of these things would just turn her into part of the opposition in his life. Also, she had no right, for she had never had anything like that happen to her, she couldn't know how it felt. She glance at the envelopes again. "How does your aunt feel?"

"She's his sister. She knows he's weak, but she's used to that, and she's of a mind that I should make up. She would, Jimmy would, but I just can't." He looked at her. What were his eyes asking her to say? "Would you, Laura?"

"Oh, Burt, I couldn't guess. Nobody could who hadn't been through it. You want to forgive him in a way, don't you?"

"In a way. I'd like it never to have happened, but then, maybe, I'd never have seen Aunt Jo and Uncle Pat, and they've been wonderful. I mean, Pat's been dead six years, but he was a good father to me, But I can't just go and pretend it doesn't matter. That would seem weak."

She touched the envelope again. "Could you put this off?"

"No. For ten years he's been sending little nothing letters. How are you doing, we're all fine here. Now, he's brought the real thing out into the open, and I can't just not deal with it. Maybe tonight, over there," and he jerked his head towards the mine, "I'll worry that I've been too harsh, too final, but those are just worry thoughts. Time to move on, and every shift is another couple of dollars closer to that ranch."

There was silence between them, and it widened. She glanced up at the clock, a big eight-sided railway clock with Roman numerals. It was almost seven. The second sitting in the dining room would be seven-thirty. Now she felt nervous sitting there with him, as if there were a tightness in him, a tension which might let slip. A picture came into her mind, a day two years ago when she and her father had sat helplessly on their horses on one side of a coulee, and watched a landslip start, right above three steers, saw it slide down and engulf the animals, They'd found only one, half-buried and dying. Her father had said that the fault was built right in, that there was no way to predict when a bit too much rain would seep down and lubricate the fault just enough to have it let go to the tug of gravity. Whatever the forces in Burt, she was not going to give the push to lubricate the fault with either advice or sympathy. Time to change the subject.

"Would you carry on with your other plan. I mean, writing to me down in Pincher Creek?"

"More than ever. I'm going to miss you, Laura."

"I'll miss you too, Burt. I hope we see each other before you go west to your ranch." He was more like her than she had thought, for he wanted the open air, the clean space. Maybe someday...

She was searching crevices of experience for something else to say when she was saved. Gerry's voice came from the door behind her. "So you did find her!"

Burt jumped up. "We were just talking." He was so emphatic that Laura giggled, the tension of the last ten minutes draining from her in a burst.

"And in a hotel lobby! Isn't that almost sinful, Gerry?"

"Maybe, if it keeps us from our dinner. Will you join us, Burt?

Burt raised both hands. "That wouldn't be right, Laura's last night. You probably have a lot to talk about."

She wanted him to stay. "Not at all. Gerry ran out of conversation on February fifteenth, and I've been mostly talking to myself since then. So come on. You didn't eat at the boarding house?"

"No, I didn't. Bully beef night, and when I smelled it cooking, I decided I wasn't hungry. Are you sure I won't be in the way?"

"Of course not," Gerry put in. "My idea, my treat." They began a good-natured argument as Laura swept ahead of them into the dining room. Mrs. Manual was German, and her larded venison was famous throughout the Crowsnest Pass.

Burt shook out a napkin. "A civilized meal! Linen!, Silverware! It's like a big CP hotel, isn't it?"

"Once or twice a year, but the occasion is important." Gerry raised his glass of water. "Going to miss you, Laura."

Burt had his glass up too, and Laura reddened. "You're going to miss my tidying up, not my nagging."

Gerry smiled. "Yes, even that. It's going to be pretty quiet in that house. Maybe I should get Burt to move in, share expenses."

Burt looked at him, surprised. "I wouldn't be much company, sleeping most of the day."

"Can you cook. That's the real question."

"For a fact, yes I can. Camp cookery mostly, but I do know my way around a kitchen. Aunt Jo runs a boarding house for about eight men, and when she wasn't able, I had to get food to the table."

Gerry grinned at Laura. "There you go, little sister. Maybe I won't miss you all that much after all."

"Oh, I can just see you two lunks in that house, littering the floor with everything you own." This banter was more fun, and she was brightening inside. "Why, Lillian Clark says …" She stopped, realizing that she was revealing the quizzing of Lillian about Burt. But the statement passed unremarked. By the time dinner was over, it was settled that Burt would move his things over on Sunday.

Three hours later, she was in the trundle bed up in the hotel room, looking at a window that allowed a band of street light up to the ceiling. Out on the flats east of Gold Creek, dark was dark, inky if there was no moon. Here in town, the lights of the street stayed on all night. Burt was nice, she thought, and it would be good for Gerry to have someone there. They liked each other. Maybe Gerry <u>would</u> invite him down to Pincher Creek, maybe even in May, for the Queen's birthday. The old lady was dead now, but they still had the holiday last year just as if she were alive. When was the new king's birthday, she wondered. Would they have another holiday?

It was midnight. Burt would have met with his shift, and they would be underground by now. When he came out in the morning, her train would be far to the east. She'd probably wake up when the Spokane Flyer came through around 5 AM, for its whistle woke her every night, just momentarily. Her train would arrive from the west about two hours later. Gerry had arranged for breakfast at 5:30. Suddenly she thought that she would miss Frank, this funny little rough town, and Gerry. And Burt.

Chapter 5

The still air was cold outside the mine office building on Dominion Street. Burt saw his breath mist into the air and disappear. He glanced down the street towards the Frank Hotel, where light still streamed from the lobby doors. The dining room was dark now. Gerry and Laura were probably sound asleep upstairs. The dinner had been fun, and he liked both of them. Would he like Gerry so much if he weren't Laura's brother? Would pigs fly if they had big enough wings? She was a girl, and he'd not had much time to think about girls; it was almost as if there was a chapter in his life, well into the future, with a door marked "Girls", and he just hadn't gotten there yet because there were other things to do, to be dealt with. But tonight he had been acutely aware of Laura as a young woman, one who seemed to like him, to want to be with him. And him? He had felt more alive, just sitting there with her. When he'd shaken hands with Gerry, saying he'd bring some things over on Friday, Laura had been standing with her hands clasped behind her back. He had turned to her, and had almost been swept up with an impulse to put his arms around her, give her a hug. Then he'd looked down and put his hand out, to receive her hand. It seemed small, smaller than the other times he'd shaken hands with her, maybe because it was limp .. no, not limp, but trusting, gentle in his hand.

He shook himself and exhaled, sending a long tendril of mist into the air. Time for work. Joe Chapman had a list in his hand that he'd been checking off. Burt counted around the circle of men. Sixteen of the twenty here so far and it was only a minute or two before midnight. Charlie Farrell came along, with the new man, a fellow who looked a little white, maybe still scared of the mine. Charlie was a great one for jollying people along. He'd be helping the boy for the next week, getting him used to joking and laughing even with a big mountain sitting on top of him. Most new men started with the day shift, where the shift bosses and foremen could keep on top of them. This new man knew something about electricity, and he'd been wiring, not filling a shovel thousands of times a day, getting the coal into a car.

Joe Chapman was square and hard, with arms that jutted out from his body, the muscles too developed to allow a normal downward swing. His legs were what people called "bandy", not just bowed like a cowboy's, but set always a little apart, and looking tense. His hair, close cropped, was curled tightly to his scalp, black with salt and pepper near his ears. Burt liked working for Joe, because the man gave him a sense of trust: I know you can do this, young fellow, and I'm going to leave you to it without forever checking. He'd be ashamed if Joe ever came to look at completed work and found shoddiness, or, worse, lack of safety. Joe was from Wales. Pat Garrity would have said, "Taffy, but still Brit — you can't trust anyone east of the Irish Sea." That was joking, Burt knew, because Pat had good friends from what he called the Big Isle. Lord knows, there were plenty of Brits in the Territory, and in the States as well, trying to be cowboys and, most of them, failing. Mining was something else. Whenever Burt entered the adit, he felt weakened, conscious of half a mile of rock suspended above his soft felt hat. But men like Joe Chapman seemed to grow in the darkness of the mine. It wasn't just the glow of carbide lamps throwing the big square shadows of the smaller square man on the black, uneven walls of the big station just inside the adit. It was a confidence, a sense that this man had just come into his natural environment, that he knew the coal, the rock, the mountain above them just as a rancher would know the draws, the coulees, the bluffs, the sloughs, the sun and the grass of his own ranch.

The last two men arrived. One almost stumbled off the wooden duckboards of the sidewalk, and Joe Chapman threw him a swift look. Burt knew that on the way to the bridge spanning the Old Man, Joe would be beside that man, assessing, judging. If the man was in drink, he would peel off, return to town, sent home sick, no work or pay that night. If it happened again, he would be given his ticket, gone from the mine. Joe wouldn't pass problem workers over to the day shift, and he would never expose his own men to the danger of working in a mine with a man who was drunk.

"Let's go then." William Warrington and Alex Clark shouldered their sacks and stepped out. Dan McKenzie followed them. He was tall and somewhat stooped. Burt sometimes wondered how a man so tall had gone into coal mining, or how he ever saw through those round steel rimmed spectacles once in the dusty mine. Dan was from Nova Scotia. He'd told Burt a month before that working under a mountain was easy compared to working under the Atlantic Ocean. "Mountains shift and groan a bit, but have you ever seen the sea, lad? All the time shifting, and you know she'll be in on you so fast if something goes wrong, so fast you'll be sucking salt water on your second breath after whatever it was happened. No, give me rock above, good footing and coal in the face, and I'll be just fine."

Shorty Dawson walked beside Burt. "How're them boots? Look damn near new, maybe I shoulda kept them 'n saved a bunch of money. These damn things I bought pinch every side. Think I shoulda told them I was a ten? Usta be a nine and a half, so that's what I told them. Spozedta stretch, d'ye think? Better do it soon, don't know what's gonna give in first, boots or feet." Burt thought about the boots he was wearing, Shorty's two weeks before, now his... They felt, well, if you don't know how a boot feels in its fit, then you don't have to think about it. Must fit fine if I don't feel them fitting badly. Shorty would carry on his monologue all night, talking to the mine horses.

Tonight he was going to work on timbering, he knew, because Mr. Warrington had put in a bid for his help, and Joe Chapman went along with the building of a team. But shortly after three, he'd be helping Shorty with the mine horses, getting them out for watering and a feed.

Gold Creek rushed below them as they crossed the first bridge, two by two on the manway beside the railway tracks of the mine spur line. A few yards farther along, the longer bridge crossed the Oldman River. Now one could feel Turtle Mountain, not just as a blacker mass in the dark night, but as a presence. A hundred and fifty yards ahead was the light of the tipple just outside the adit, and below, perched between the tipple and the river, the lighted windows of the power plant. They trudged along, silent mountain to their right, sibilant river to their left. There were a few winks of light, kerosene lanterns behind windows of homes on the flats. Burt squinted, trying to guess where Gerry's home would be from this angle, but knowing it was certainly dark. There were some points of light to the northeast, campfires, perhaps half a mile east of the shoe shop. That would be the camp of the railway construction workers, the McVeigh and Poupore camp right beside the CPR main line. Beyond the fires, only darkness. There was a ranch that way, he knew, and a few homes up the northeast slope of the Crows Nest Valley, but everything was dark. Twisting around, he could see the lights of Dominion Street.

The miners crossed the tracks to walk beside the line of coal cars and lost sight of the town. Finally, they climbed the wooden steps up to the adit level.

Alex Tashigan stopped by the tipple. He would work out here tonight, weighing and dumping the last coal cars left by the day shift, washing down the coal as it slid into the railway cars below. Five full cars were spotted downgrade from the tipple, and one car sat below it, almost full. Tashigan would finish it in an hour or two, then wash down the scales. Maybe the CPR agent would be sending an engine up the mine spur tonight.

The others stopped just inside the adit to light their safety lamps. Burt thumbed the screw which allowed a water drip into the dry carbide, and soon heard the hiss of acetylene. The flint wheel lit the gas and the mantle began to glow. Burt capped the mantle with its cover. Joe Chapman walked along the line looking at each lamp. Two young men had been killed in an explosion six months back because they used open flame lamps. The man who had seemed unsteady back in town must have passed Joe's inspection, for Burt saw him fixing his lamp to the broad brimmed felt hat.

He remembered the explosion. It had been a fairly small one, for the two young miners had entered a few minutes before the scheduled start of the day shift, and there would not have been much dust in the air. Most of the miners figured they were using open flame lamps. There were still some of those around, and they were easy to light and relight. Joe Chapman wouldn't allow them on his shift, but some of the other foremen were not as sharp eyed. Every miner in town had known of the "bump" within a half-hour of it happening. Night men who had just tumbled into bed were woken, for they might be needed. Some of the men arriving for work had been knocked down by the blast, but were on their feet in seconds, running in to help.

That had been the start of several months of nervousness in the mine. One night, workers checking a mined out seam found that it had shrunk from over six feet to a few inches. Dan McKenzie, inspecting the workings that night, had said the mountain had moved a bit. "That's how mountains got here in the first place, lad. Movement. You don't think this coal got started in an up and down seam like this, do you? No, the mountain moved her up here, and I don't think the mountain's going to stop moving just because a bunch of us ants are tunnelling away in her. Moves even slower than an Upper Canadian, so I reckon it's pretty safe."

That was Dan's usual attitude, and Burt would have been more ready to accept it if he hadn't seen the split stall three days later. A butt end of Ponderosa Pine, two and a half feet in diameter, was compressed between two rock walls so much that splinters stood out three feet on all sides. Further up the mine, one timber had been totally crushed, and timbers on both sides had been broken, bent or been contemptuously shoved aside for fifty yards each way. Once Burt had found tracks laid the night before, tracks which had been straight twenty hours earlier, twisted into a crazy S bend. Seventy yards away, the tracks ended a good foot to the right of their continuation. Everybody had their tales of things moving in the mountain, but the stories had trailed off in January. If the mountain had moved, it seemed to have stopped its wandering.

William Warrington nodded to Burt and Shorty, and they peeled off to follow him. The night shift men all knew what they were doing and where, and there were few words. Mr. Warrington would take his three man team on a full tour of the mine, looking at the timbering, the stalls, the platform supports, the chutes. As they climbed the first series of ladders, Burt thought about how strange it was that we emptied out the coal, this stuff that had been compressed into almost rock hardness, and we replaced it with air and a lattice of wood, artfully angled to hold space open. Four hundred yards in from the opening of the adit, the first of three huge chutes went up to an immense mined out chamber, half a mile long, fifteen feet wide and two hundred and fifty feet high, most of it filled with broken coal. The stopers on the day shift would work from the surface of the broken coal, cutting upwards into the seam. The manway the three men were climbing ladders in was in the centre of a pillar of solid, unbroken coal, with crosscuts leading off to both sides every twenty feet or so. It was the timbering in these crosscuts that had to be checked. The pillar itself was about forty feet wide, providing one of eight partitions in the chamber.

As Warrington paused above him, Burt's lamp cast the shadow of a ladder rung on the coal surface. It looked solid and reliable, but a pick would sink into it a foot. Ten feet behind him was the interface where the coal seam met the limestone of Turtle Mountain. Twenty feet to his left was the edge of the pillar, where hundreds of tons of broken coal waited to be drawn down through the chute and fed into the waiting cars.

This chamber was the biggest in the mine. Farther up the big drift tunnel, two more chutes went upwards to chambers that were just beginning to be mined. The last chute was a mile from the opening of the adit. Burt wondered if anyone had the whole picture of the mine in his head. For him, the mine was always that cone of light projected by his safety lamp, a cone that went out to be swallowed by black walls, dust, wet wood, and nothingness.

They followed William Warrington into the darkness of a crosscut. He was checking the timbering where it had been put in, well over a year ago. His lamp swept around the ends of each timber stall, looking at its placement, the wedges holding it in place and then along its length, looking for compression fractures. There was one stall he didn't like early on. It had a pronounced bow in it, and some splinters already appearing on the top edge where it bowed upwards. He measured it quickly and spoke to Shorty, who disappeared down the ladders to fetch a new stall. Then Warrington spoke to Burt. "See this wedge, lad? Bad place to put it, surprised I never noticed before. Not too important, but if the stall slipped out because of the placement, that would be important. The wall's moving in a bit, and we'll have to put something in to hold her back."

He and Burt went on. They checked the level of a platform used to deflect falling coal from the manway. It had come away from the wall a foot or so, and Warrington hammered a timber down to lever the platform back. Burt wedged it into place. They retreated to the ladder, and Burt descended to fetch a coil of rope. Shorty would be back with the new stall, and they would have to haul it up. As he emerged from the manway at the main level, there was Shorty's lamp coming up the adit. Burt slung the rope around his shoulder and started up the ladders again to where Warrington would rig the block. Again, he was alone, just himself and the ladder, shadows of the rungs jerking downwards. If his lamp were to go out, he would be in total darkness, so complete that if he held his hand in front of his face, he would feel its heat, but not see it.. But not silence, no, for the mine was never quiet. There was always a faint creak, a small tick through the coal, a sighing of air from the ventilation shafts as if the mountain were breathing, trying out its man-made lungs, preparatory to stretching and flexing its muscles.

A coil of the rope snagged on a projecting rung, and his left hand almost slipped from the rung above. He leaned into the ladder. If he had fallen, it would only have been a few feet to the platform he had just left; at worst, he would have snapped a bone or sprained something. But he was alone for the moment. The team of three had been forced to part for the needs of the job, Warrington fifty feet up, Shorty down below, him in between with the connecting rope. For miners, the need to stay in sight of a partner was almost like the need for air. The most solitary hermit in the world above would clutch at companionship down here. He took two deep breaths and started to climb again. In two minutes he was handing the rope to Warrington.

Fifteen minutes later, the new stall was in place, a piece of lodgepole pine eighteen inches in diameter telling the mountain not to move any more. The three men moved on, eventually going down the last manway in the chamber. When they reached the adit level, they saw three lamps coming from deeper in the mine. Warrington checked his watch. "Right on time. All right, lads, you get on with the horses and have your nibble out under the stars. I'll meet you here in an hour or so." Burt and Shorty touched their hats as if saluting, the beams from their lamps tilting down and up again in exaggerated courtesy, and walked together towards the stables and the adit entrance. Only two of the horses would have done any work tonight, , but all the stable stalls had to be checked, water troughs filled, feed given, and a human touch bestowed. He and Shorty would take the horses out of the mine and let them eat in the open air.

Moonlight flooded the drift near the opening. It must have risen since they started the shift. Alex Tashigan was talking with two men, CPR trainmen from the look of them. Down to the left was their engine which had backed up the spur to pick up the loaded cars.

Getting the horses out was easy. Moving them back into the darkness of the mine, up that three hundred feet to their hollowed out stable was a little harder. Before the last trip, Shorty and he had their sandwiches and cold tea, sitting with Alex for a minute. The two trainmen were walking around the cars, while the driver was pacing back and forth by his engine. One of them called out to the other, but the words were lost in the vastness of the valley.

Shorty finished first, and picked up the bridle ropes of his team. "See ya inside." Charley and Burt were left on the flat surface in front of the adit entrance. Alex was washing the big chute. Burt capped his tea bottle and lit his lamp.

"Let's go, Charley." The big horse shuddered and breathed a long fluttering sigh. The moonlight shrank behind them, and Burt's cone of light brightened before them. As they neared the stable, another light appeared in the tunnel. Charley's stall was at the far end of the stable, but the horse was reluctant to go into it, so Burt took him past, fifty feet farther into the mine. Charley might look on the stall as more friendly if approached from that direction. Just as he was turning the horse around, he heard Joe Chapman's voice.

"That you, Delaney?"

Joe's voice, but it might have been the hand of God that struck before he could answer. A roar filled the mine, the mountain, the whole world. Lifted from his feet by some unimaginable force, his body whirling in the air, he saw Charley also flying sideways. He was barely conscious of moving air because he was part of it, a leaf in the wind. His ears began to ring and his lamp was snuffed out, but still the roar went on. His body slammed to the floor, and he was conscious of ties and rails as he rolled. Then silence.

Chapter 6

The noise that woke her was incredibly loud, and it went on and on. The trundle bed rolled across the shaking floor and bounced off the wall, dumping her and her blankets. Was the building collapsing? As she thought this, the window exploded inwards scattering glass across the floor. She struggled to get clear of her blankets. The room was filling with something, smoke or dust, pouring in the window with a strong east wind, and still the roaring noise continued.

It stopped suddenly. An isolated thump, then two more close together, then silence. The dust in the air stopped its rush, quivered back and forth, and stilled as the wind ceased and the curtain fell straight. By now, she was struggling to her feet in the darkness. No yellow light from street lamps came through the window, just a pearly, unreal glow.

"Laura." Gerry's voice sounded doubtful, panicky.

"I'm here, Gerry. What's happening?"

"Oh, good. The building's still standing. I thought it was falling down. I'll see if I can get some light. Stay where you are."

She heard him fumbling around on the big old bureau near the door. A woman was crying somewhere, and she could hear shouting out on the street. She took a deep breath, and coughed from the dust. Now she could see that the moon must be up. Gerry struck a safety match and found the lantern where it had fallen.

In another few seconds it was glowing. Gerry said, "I think we'd better get out on the street. The hotel was shaking pretty hard, and it might be dangerous to stay here."

Laura was already dressing. Her travelling clothes were hanging on a nail, with her heavy tweed coat on another nail. "What time is it, Gerry?"

"Quarter past four. I wonder what that god awful noise was. Are you all right?"

"Almost deaf, that's all. I'm ready."

The fireplace in the lobby was still glowing as they came down the stairs. One man rushed past them, dressed in a long nightshirt that almost tripped him on the bottom step. He was whimpering like a whipped dog.

Outside, the street was filled with people some running into the street from the east. Laura was shoved violently from behind, and she whirled to see a woman, a young woman only a year or so older than herself, who had run into her. The woman was crying, holding on to a bundle that Laura suddenly realized was a baby. Both were in nightclothes. Laura unbuttoned her tweed coat, shook it off, and wrapped it around the woman, who looked surprised, then said, "Thank you, oh, thank you." before turning down the street towards the station. Laura looked at her coat disappearing down the street, then thought of her suitcase upstairs. Should she go and get it now, so she'd be ready when her train came? Then she knew that she wouldn't be leaving Frank today, that whatever had happened was so big that normal life was suspended.

Gerry was carrying a lantern, and so were many other men. Some were wearing miner's hats with headlamps. Gerry grabbed one by the arm. "Harold, what's going on? Does anybody know?"

"Must be the mine. Helluva big bump. Never heard nothing like it, and I've been mining fifteen years. I was sleeping over in the boarding house, and the whole damn building lifted up, it felt like. There's a big cloud over the whole valley, but no explosive smell, nor coal gas. If it was a bump, it sure don't smell like one."

Another man interrupted, pushing between Gerry and Laura. "It's no mine explosion. It's what they call an earth-quaker. This town's going to get shaken right down." Laura realized that they were going to get as many theories as there were people to talk to. She pulled Gerry's sleeve and they backed out of the group.

"Maybe we should go down to the station, Gerry. They've got the telegraph there, and maybe there's news from outside. Come to think of it, we could find out about trains, too." Gerry nodded, and they started up Dominion towards the station, turning right on the street that ended at the trestle over Gold Creek. Gerry still had the lantern and it showed a few feet of ground in front of them. To either side, buildings were ghostly in the dust and the moonlight.

Gerry stopped suddenly. "My God, Laura! Look at that!" They were facing the creek, but it had lost all familiarity. A bank of mud separated them from the water, the mud steaming with heat even as the icy creek trickled through it. On the other side, the moonlight showed more mud, and then some huge chunks of rock piled up as if some giant baby had gotten tired of building something and had knocked the pile of blocks down. Deep in the murk of the dust, they could see the glow of a fire, but it was impossible to tell how far away it was.

"It can't have been the mine, Gerry. Look at that rock. The mine's way over in the mountain." For the first time, she thought about Burt. Why hadn't she thought of him when they were talking about a mine explosion? But she'd been moving ever since she was thrown out of bed an hour ago. However, she was glad that the mine probably wasn't involved. Burt would be coming out in a few hours, and he'd be surprised at what had happened here, and he'd be glad she wasn't hurt.

To their left, they could see some lanterns swinging, blinking on and off as their bearers started into the huge rocks. Gerry looked at her sadly. "Laura, the rocks had to come from somewhere, and that has to be the mountain. Turtle Mountain, not the north side of the valley. But it didn't start with the mine, it's a lot bigger than that. Come on, let's get over to the station." As they got closer, they could see that a good part of Frank's population was gathering there Carbide lamps glinted from dark figures, and a number of lanterns were raised with outstretched arms.

"There's Rob Leard," Gerry said. The NWMP constable wore a dark greatcoat and a fur cap, and it was only the reflected flash from his cap badge that identified him.

"Now be quiet, and let's sort this thing out," they heard him shout. "The telegraph's out to the east, but I've let Cranbrook know that something has happened here. Now, I don't know exactly what's going on, but there's an engineer here, Mr. Murgatroyd, who has some idea. I'd suggest that we all close our yaps and let him say what he knows."

The engineer was a stout, middle-aged man with huge moustaches blending into his sideburns, and eyebrows that met over his nose as if they were trying to bridge his face as luxuriantly as the hair below. "We was just spotting a car up to the mine, after we took away the cars they had waiting. Just got her rolling with me brakemen walking along beside, and a big chunk of rock clunked down on the left side and bounced clear over the engine. Then another, and in a minute it was raining rocks out there. Choquette and Lowes, they jumped on the engine, cause I already had her churning to get out of there. We made it over the bridge, but it got taken out right behind us. We got here, and then we see there's rock on the main line."

A taller man in the uniform of a CPR conductor, tapped Constable Leard's shoulder and whispered to him. Leard gestured for him to speak to the crowd. "My name's Pettit. We laid our train by here, 'cause the Spokane Flyer's running late. But she's due any minute, and if she comes running up into that rock pile out there, there'll be a lot of people hurt, probably killed. So I sent Choquette and his partner out over the blockage to try to flag down the Flyer. Judging by the noise, it was a big slide. We'll be able to see better when the sun comes up."

The last statement set the crowd murmuring. Gerry looked at his watch. Ten to six, an hour and thirty or forty minutes since the huge noise filled the valley. In that short time, the first confused guesses about the event had hardened into firm convictions, some arguing that it was the Second Coming, others sticking to the mine explosion theory, a few maintaining that the sudden blast of wind had caused the rockfalls. From here, high on the embankment west of the trestle, Laura could see that there were several small fires burning, mostly close to Gold Creek. Some of the dust cloud was settling now. Down valley, dawn was showing red and purple, and the light was growing stronger by the minute. People began to fall silent, and soon the whole crowd was facing east.

"Oh, my God!"

The sun, invisible to the crowd was catching the top of the mountain on the north side of the pass. An immense jumble of rock cubes, white and smoking with its own dust, extended over a mile past the railway it buried, up five hundred feet over the watchers. One block detached itself lazily from the top edge of the jumble and rolled down two or three hundred feet. Farther over to the east, a small slide started down the slope and then petered out.

The one speaker had said it all for the crowd. It seemed that only the hand of God could have delivered a blow like this. Some kept staring at the rock still quivering in its resting place up the far valley side. Most turned to peer into the darkness which continued to fill the lower part of the valley. As far as the eye could see, there was rock. Laura moved closer to Gerry, and he put his arm around her shoulder. The town, as they swung their gaze that way, was darker than usual, with no street lights, but it was alive with small flickering points of light. She could see people moving down to the creek with lanterns, but on the other side of the creek there were few lights. She should have been able to see the mine entrance and the power plant, always brilliantly lit even after sunrise. But there was nothing there. Across the trestle, the tracks disappeared into the rock pile. Less than a mile farther on, she realized with a shudder, was the house, the shoe shop, where she had lived for the past months, Gerry's home and livelihood. Now there was a vast expanse of rubble.

A light flickered a hundred feet north of the point where the tracks disappeared, and a man stumbled towards them. "It's Lowes!" Mr. Pettit's authoritative voice announced. "Help him, some of you there." Three men detached themselves from the crowd and ran to help the staggering man. He was carried across the trestle.

"It's ... ah, uh, uh, uh..."

"Easy, man, catch your breath."

Lowes gulped the air in great sobs, his breath whistling in. His breathing slowed and steadied. "I couldn't go on, it's so huge." He breathed four or five more times. "Sid, he's younger, he kept on, but it looked like it was going to go on forever. I saw your lights when I got up a big block, but Sid, he's got nothing to go by. Anyway, my chest, I couldn't breathe right, and I had to quit. Sid said to go back, tell people it's so big."

Laura looked down the valley. The sun was definitely coming up now, though it was still behind the mountains. Square miles of rock smoked before her. Somewhere in that ruin, a man was trying to squirm through to stop a train. Somewhere below the tons of rock lay people she knew. Florence and her young man. Lillian Clark was probably under rock only a few hundred yards away. The men at the livery stable. Women she'd waved to, not knowing their names. No one could look at the expanse of rubble and hope. Except maybe along the edges. She grabbed Gerry's arm. "Gerry, there might be people alive, not way out there, but close. Can we do something?"

"Look at the creek, Laura." The creek was widening as they watched. "It must be dammed by the slide, or the river is," Gerry said, "but, look, there's someone wading it." Two figures were waist deep in the water, leaning and struggling to get through the stream. Laura stepped down the embankment holding on to one piling of the trestle, then picked her way along the edge of the dark water. Gerry called to her once, then followed.

Laura was holding one figure when he caught up to her. He stepped into the water and grasped the extended hand of a teen-aged boy. "It's Ruby and Tom. Come on, Ruby, let's get you into a house. Or the hotel, it's not far."

"The house, something knocked it down. Have you seen Mama? We couldn't find her, or Fernie. Then we saw the lights. There's rock everywhere. The Ackroyds' house is burning, and the Leitchs', there's just the roof, sitting by the creek. That's all we could see. What happened?" Ruby Watkins was a year younger than her brother, but a few inches taller. Laura continued to pull her along, conscious of the cold for the first time since she gave her coat away. Gerry was supporting Tom, whose sobbing matched their pace.

"There's searchers over there now." Looking back, Laura could see there were now dozens of people swarming over the edge of the rock expanse. "They'll find them. Are you hurt?"

Ruby shook her head. "Just cold. And scared. Tom and me, when we woke up, and the house wasn't there, just a bunch of boards and mud and rocks. We heard someone calling and we tried to get to the voice, but we got confused, you can't find your way, and it was still dark. Even after we saw the town, it was hard keeping going in the right direction."

The hotel lobby was jammed with people. They took Ruby and Tom up to their room. Laura dug into her suitcase, getting out sweaters and some riding pants; perhaps the fit wouldn't be right, but they were dry. Gerry couldn't help much, for he'd brought only a few little things, expecting to go to his house after Laura was on the train. On the train! It seemed laughable now, the tracks maybe twenty feet under all that rock.

Young Tom was quieting now. Ruby looked at her new finery. "Thanks, Miss Freeman. I guess my own clothes are gone for good now. I just hope that Mama and Fernie … but Dad'll be all right, 'cause he was on the night shift. I guess they'll be out by now." Gerry and Laura looked at each other. Things were coming together; all that rock had to come from somewhere, and it obviously had come from the south. It looked like half of Turtle Mountain was spread across the valley. Were the miners also spread across the valley, or were they still inside what was left of the mountain?

Laura hugged Ruby and patted her back. "I'm sure he'll be fine, Ruby, but probably he'll be awfully busy for a while. We'll make sure he gets the message about where you are, and when we find your mother and Fernie, we'll bring them here. You lie down for a bit, and if we're not here when you wake, it'll be because we're out trying to find people. You'll be safe here."

The two watched them as Gerry stuffed a pillow in the window. Laura was thinking hard. Who else was on that night shift? Burt Delaney of course, and he'd said Mr. Warrington, then Shorty Dawson. Lillian's father, Mr. Clark would be there. Or they'd all be dead.

Chapter 7

His eyes blinked in the light. He was being shaken by the shoulders, but it was hard to work out where he was.

"Delaney! Are you with us, lad?"

Two more shakes and he knew the voice, the same as the last voice he'd heard before the blackness. Joe Chapman. "Yessir, Mr. Chapman. What happened?" The light swung away from his face.

"If I knew, I'd tell you, lad. A couple of minutes ago there was a wind in here like you wouldn't believe, and the next thing I see is this great horse flying through the air at me. Missed me, and I went for a fly myself. The horse got knocked out, I think, and when I got up and found my hat and my lamp, and got her lit, then I saw you lying here. But whatever it was set off that wind, it was big. Are you feeling all right? Let me see you move your feet."

Burt wiggled one foot, then the other. The movement didn't hurt, not particularly, since he was hurting all over, generally. He started to raise his head to look for his hat and lamp. "Easy, young fellow. Check the arms too. Are they working?" They were. Now Burt was aware that he was lying across some rails.

Joe Chapman's light swept the tunnel. "There's your hat, over by the horse. You can sit up now?" Burt rolled to his left and pushed himself up. His back felt as if the rail was still buried in it. Nothing was broken, but there was nothing that felt really right. Joe Chapman crossed over to the unconscious horse and got the hat and lamp, expertly unscrewing the carbide tank as he came back. "You're still good for an hour or two, he said, peering into the container before screwing it back onto the lamp. Start 'er up and let's see what goes down here."

Burt got his lamp going and stood up, still wobbly. Charley was lying on his side, but Burt could see the big horse's side moving in deep breaths. At least he was alive. The two men turned back toward the mine entrance, walking past the stables. "How many horses here at start of shift?" Joe's lamp picked out two horses in the stalls.

"Five. That's the pair Shorty brought in just ahead of me. There's two missing. They were out at the tipple."

"That's right. Alex Clark and Fred Farrington would have been using them. Did you see them?"

"No, we—Shorty and me—we were just out there for a few minutes. Maybe Alex and Fred were down the steps with their lunch. I saw Tashigan washing down the scales." Burt looked back up the tunnel. Lamps were coming down, and a babble of voices filled the air. By now, he and Joe Chapman had come to a dead end, the tunnel completely blocked with huge chunks of rock. Soon they were surrounded with men.

"Look at that!"

"Must be sixty feet of the tunnel blocked!"

"Look at the rock. It's not from right above, that's all shale and coal. This is hard rock, not just a cave in."

"And it's no sixty feet. It's more like three hundred to the entrance."

Joe Chapman's authority cut the off. "First things first. Let's see who's here. Circle up." The men shuffled into a circle, and Clark went around, saying each man's name. "That's it, I think. Seventeen of us here. Clark, Farrington, Tashigan all out at the entrance, and we don't know if they are hurt or not. Anybody here hurt?"

William Warrington's voice was weak. "My leg caught it. I was in a narrow spot when the bump came, and the drift moved. Think it's broken."

"Get some straw, you two." Two miners headed for the stable on Chapman's order. "Will, you just lie here. Take it easy. The rest of us will go down to the lower manway and see if there's a way out there. If there is, two of us will be back with a stretcher."

Sixteen men went in single file back to the manway, and started down ladders. Burt was fourth in line, and he'd just stepped off the third ladder when a shout from below stopped him. "Hold it, up there! The manway's got water in her. Back off. There's no way out here. I'll stay here a bit and see if it's sinking or rising." Soon fifteen men were back at the main tunnel. After a few minutes, Joe Chapman emerged.

"The water's rising, lads, not too quickly, but who knows whether it will keep coming up, or drain. But we'd be fools to wait and see if we could get out that way. Let's get back to Will."

"How fast is it filling?" This was Dan McKenzie.

"About six inches in the couple of minutes I was watching. I don't know if a spring got opened or what."

"Might it be the river?"

"We're a good height above flood stage for the river. But it's got to be something, 'cause it's more than normal drainage by a long shot."

When the group was once more gathered around William Warrington on his bed of straw, Joe Chapman had all but three turn off their lamps. "If the air shafts got pinched off, we'll need all the air we can get. And there may be gas farther up. Dan, take Shorty and John, get up to the old Nicholson level. You know the way?" McKenzie nodded, the movement of his lamp beam making the shadows of the circled men dance wildly on the tunnel walls. "Check the air shafts from there. We'll see if we can move some of this out. The rest of you, get your tools. One lamp per pair."

During the next hour Burt began to feel the kind of paralyzing fear that a trapped animal must feel. He'd often asked Pat Garrity about war, and Pat had talked about fear as something that came after danger more often than during it. Here in the dark mine, men worked desperately at a tangle of rock and timber, prying chunks loose, hammering with fierce energy at blocks too large to dislodge. Burt could see that a yard per hour was the most they could make, maybe fifty hours to freedom at the very best. Water coming up from below, maybe gas from above, the oxygen in the air dropping with every gasp of labouring men — this was hopeless. Probably Joe Chapman knew it was hopeless, but was keeping panic at bay with activity.

Presently the three men returned from the ladders. "No hope there, Joe," Dan McKenzie said. "Air shafts completely blocked and some gas, too. How's it look here?"

Chapman just shook his head. The men at the face of the blockage stopped working. Burt pulled out his watch and leaned forward to put it in front of another man's lamp. Seven eighteen, a little over three hours since the bump or whatever it was. How long would the air last? He heard Joe Chapman say, "Take a break." a minute after the last pick had been swung. Could Joe keep his authority if hope was sinking? Two more lights were snuffed, and now there were only two left, one by William Warrington's bed, and the other near the face. At the edge of the aura, three figures detached from the group and moved forty feet up tunnel. One was Joe Chapman, another Dan McKenzie. They were in conference.

Burt leaned back against the wall of the tunnel. It was strange— in a way he'd been mentally prepared for an accident in the mine, a sudden cave-in crushing the life from him before he could even cry out, an explosion smearing him across a rock wall, even a sudden choking death. All were possibilities, chances, things to be accepted and shoved to the back of his mind. But not this. Not just sitting here, unhurt, waiting for water to drown him, or gas to choke him, or just to sit here between the two and go to sleep because there wasn't enough air to keep him alive, and so to die. Not eighteen yet, no ranch of his own, never to be able to pull Aunt Jo and Jimmy out of that boarding house in Macleod. Never to see Laura, his sister. He shook his head. What did he mean? He'd never have seen his sister again, anyway. Maybe his mind was playing tricks on him, maybe he'd been thinking of Laura Freeman, now on her way to Pincher Creek carrying his letters with her.

The man next to him shifted and grunted. Was that Shorty? No, taller, probably Alex Grant. How much did he know of these men, now that they were in their common grave? Not much, he realized. He respected some of them, but they were still mainly figures he saw in the dark of midnight, and parted with after dawn, but didn't know. If only Pat Garrity were here! He leaned his head back and closed his eyes, trying to recover the warm sunshine of Montana in the summer, the old soldier beside him on the fence rail, the lilting Irish voice. Telling him…telling him what? He grimaced. The last thing he remembered Pat telling him was not to be angry at his father. The same thing Aunt Jo had said in her letter. And it was the last thing he was interested in thinking about. So he'd made sure of cutting that thread with his letter, cutting off with him, with Laura, oh, and sure, the hated Grace.

"Boy, you sure do it completely when you decide to mess up," he said aloud.

. The man next to him—yes, it was Alex Grant—turned to ask, "What's that, son?"

"Nothing, Mr. Grant. Just got thinking."

"Praying's more to the point, unless you're thinking of a way out. One that works."

Burt wondered if there was a way of changing things, perhaps leaving a message somehow (in here?) for his father and for Laura. But who would find it, and what would it count? His father's letter had been stiff, dignified, something he'd read through a red film of anger. Sitting here on a rock in the dark, he could sense something else, a sorrow. How many letters in the past few years had he read and crumpled without really trying to feel what the writer meant?

Deathbed conversion, he thought wryly. Only now, between water and gas, trapped in rock, do I decide to become a nice forgiving sort. That letter from Minneapolis had talked about things going well in business. Would he come back east and they'd talk things over. Could he bring Jimmy? Would he like to learn the hardware business?

He knew very well that he didn't want to learn the hardware business, but it was pride that made him reject the offer. Now he was inside a black mountain, soon to be gasping for life.

A third lamp flared into life, and he heard an angry murmur to shut that damned thing off, don't you like to breathe? Dan McKenzie's voice cut in. "Joe's gone up to check something. Anybody remember an outcrop of coal up above the adit, and over to the left if you're facing the mountain?"

"Yeah. Climbed up that way once. Bit of dirt and lichen on her, but there's maybe fifty feet, ten, twelve feet wide, runs from an overhang down ... well, like I say, fifty feet." A tired voice that Burt didn't recognize.

Dan answered. "That's what we thought. Maybe we can get at that seam from the inside. How far above the adit?"

"'Bout a hundred and fifty feet, not two hundred." There was a stir among the men. Burt realized that the watch was still in his hand. It was almost 8:30.

"It'll be close work, and not much room to drop the coal, so we can't have more than two or three working at the same time. Let's have six come with me now, and when the first team's tired, we'll get some more up there." Dan named six men, Burt among them. It was a relief to get moving, to be doing something. Four and a half hours after the bump. A pick slung through his belt, more ladders, and they met Joe Chapman.

Dan told Joe what the man below had said. "Sounds right to me," Joe replied. "The seam here is pretty narrow, not worth working for the coal. But if it don't peter out, it shouldn't be too far to the face of the mountain. But I'm not dead sure, not within a hundred feet. And who's to say the seam's continuous? But it don't look like we've got many choices. Fine, now, you three start in here and keep it in line this way." He gestured with his arm. "The other three, sit and keep quiet. Breathe only if you have to. No lamps, except one at the face."

Two men began swinging picks while the third worked to clear the coal away from their feet. Burt watched, then closed his eyes. Time enough when it was his turn. The steady "chunk, chink" of the picks and the rattle of coal on the shovel, the grunts of exertion, all mingled into a sort of metronome, a;most a clock-like ticking, measuring the time until air was met or air was gone. It was too dark to check his watch, but it was probably twenty minutes when the sound slowed and stopped. Burt and his two partners slid past the exhausted men, Burt swapping hats and taking the lamp. Then it was swing, hit, lever, scrabbling bits of coal from the face, inching forward, feet slipping on the broken coal, muscles aching from the shortened swings. He gasped for breath, then told himself to be efficient. Only so much air, only so much time. Make every swing count. Half his lifetime was in there, shoulder against one wall, pick pulled in tight to keep clear of his partner, and he heard Joe say,"Next crew. Well done, lads."

Clear of the narrow, lengthening tunnel, he saw that all the shift was up here now, including William Warrington on a litter made of old timber splinters and some work clothes. His muscles were protesting, and he tried to relax them, slacken them to get ready for the next go round.

Joe Chapman started to get into a relay of workers, and Dan McKenzie stood in front of him. "Joe, you're in charge. Someone's got to be thinking clear, and it better be you. We've got five relays without you and Will, so you stay out of pick swinging, even if you're good at it. Some of us may be getting groggy before too long." Chapman looked at him and nodded. The work continued.

At one point, Burt realized that it was past noon. Twelve hours underground now. The air was getting worse, for he could feel himself gulping for air, trying to get more into his lungs. In the darkness, he could hear rasping breath, and he wondered when the first man would pass out. Maybe someone had already.

There was some muttering over to his right, and then a shuffle as some men got up and headed for the ladder. He saw a lamp flicker into life fifty feet away, and heard a murmur of protest from some men close to him. Why was that fool using precious air just to see where they were going? The lamp went out.

Some time later, the lamp appeared again at the manway and was extinguished. Men groped their way back to the group, found spots to sit. "Went back to check the main tunnel, figured it couldn't be worse than this idea, but it is. No way out down there. It's this way or nothing, we figure."

Then everyone was silent, and the picks worked their rhythm of shortening life, picking their inches into a dark future, while the shovel moved the past out in crumbles of coal.

Chapter 8

By ten o'clock, the Palm Restaurant was as crowded as Laura had ever seen it. Mrs. Bell bustled back and forth between kitchen and dining room, greeting people and keeping a running account of death, injury and survival on the blackboard normally used for the daily menu. Right now, the menu consisted of thick oatmeal, rashers of bacon, and gallons of hot, strong coffee. Laura wiped her forehead with a dishcloth, then started in again on the bowls in the big sink. Every couple of minutes, she would stop, wipe her hands, and go over to the range to stir the huge pot of soup that Mrs. Bell planned to switch to for lunch, just before noon. There were trays of scones baking in the oven, but Laura had been warned in very specific terms that only Mrs. Bell had the expertise to judge when they were done.

After leaving Tom and Ruby Watkins in their room, she and Gerry had come down to Dominion Avenue and realized that they were terribly hungry. The door to the Palm was open, and Mrs. Bell waved them in. "Porridge and bacon coming up!" she cried. The porridge was lumpier than Laura liked, but it was hot. The bacon was underdone. "Not the best," Mrs. Bell boomed, "but I couldn't take the time this morning. Isn't it awful? They say the rest of the mountain may be coming down any minute. Eat up!"

When Gerry's purse came out, she laughed. "Not today, young fellow. Food's free today. least we can do, so many hurt and killed.

Say, don't you live out on the eastern flats?" Gerry explained their decision to stay in town. "Lost your house, though, and your shop and all the tools, I guess. Rough."

"We feel lucky, Mrs. Bell," Laura offered. "At least that house was empty when it got covered. The sights the other side of Gold Creek ... why, they're just terrible, and the two Watkins children, Ruby and Tom, well, they've ..." Suddenly, she couldn't go on. She was staring at Gerry, and his face blurred as her eyes filled with tears. In a few seconds, she was sobbing uncontrollably. Mrs. Bell's arms were around her, and she was led through the kitchen and upstairs to the Bells' living quarters.

"You just lie there for a while, dear. A little nap wouldn't be amiss. I'll be down in the kitchen."

Fifteen minutes worked wonders. Soon, she was feeling guilty about the crashing noises from the kitchen, and made her way down to offer help. Mr. Bell was cutting up vegetables for a soup pot, and he gestured to the sink, where the porridge bowls were piling up beside stacks of plates dripping bacon grease. Soon Laura was up to her elbows in suds.

Around ten-thirty by the restaurant clock, there was a lull, and for the first time, Laura was ahead on the dishes. Until the soup got going, she thought. She started for the dining room and collided with Mrs. Bell. "Oh, dearie, I was just coming to tell you, you must have been wondering. Your brother, he's gone off to help the rescue teams over the creek. Oh, and I've had word on Mrs. Watkins. They've just brought her to Dr. Malcolmson's house, unconscious, maybe hurt bad, bleeding all over from stone splinters. Lester Johnson's there too, poor lad, a chunk of wood went right into his side, but he broke it off and swam the creek naked as a newborn mouse."

"What about the Clarks? And, oh, the Warringtons?"

"Warringtons? Oh, the family across the path from the livery stable. Nothing left, poor souls. The say the rock is twenty feet deep there. The Clarks, they were in the last of that row of cottages, weren't they? Not a sign of the cottage, dear."

At the thought of Florence and her young man lying there, Laura thought that she would start to cry again, but her outburst this morning had drained something. It must have been fast, no time between waking and dying. Death should come to someone when they've lived their life, had their children, seen them grow, when they've been old, sick, tired and ready. Of course there were premature deaths. Joey Ralston had drowned just outside Pincher Creek, and him only sixteen, her age now. But this was so much bigger, the sweep of rock and wind and mud. It was like that poem by Lord Byron about the Assyrian army being swept over by the Angel of Death. Here the Angel of Death had used half a mountain as his scythe. And poor little Lillian Clark, never got to live a real life, just work in that boarding house, and go home to a cottage to share a bed with two younger sisters.

Mrs. Bell went over to update her list of casualties, now extending past the blackboard to a pencilled list on the wallpaper. Two miners came in, one relatively clean, the other still as black as the pit. "Some porridge, lads? Still some left. Get it for them, would you, Laura?"

Laura brought out the bowls of porridge and some cold bacon, and the men began to eat. She hovered at the table. "I was wondering ..."

"Yes, Miss?" It was the dirtier of the two.

"Were you ... I mean, did you work the shift, the one that started at midnight?"

"Me? Oh, yeah, I guess I look it. No'm, I got off just after eleven last night, just never got washed or changed before I went for a few drinks, and then I got into a poker game, and... well, I was still at it when the noise came this morning. Sorry, Miss, the guys on the maintenance shift, they're still in there if they're alive at all. Me and Jack here, we been over to the spot the engineer figures is where the adit starts, and we been tearing away at some rock there, but we got no idea of how far in. And there's still some fair sized chunks bouncing down off the mountain, one damn near got me about an hour ago. Only twelve of us can work there at a time, so Jack and me got sent over for some lunch and a rest. We'll be back at 'er this afternoon."

"Don't look good, Miss," his cleaner but quieter partner added.

"Thank you," she gasped and headed for the kitchen. All those men, too. Burt Delaney, working in the dark for a ranch, and now probably dead in there, or, worse, dying a slow and horrible death. She felt as though a cold iron ball was in her stomach, and she stirred the soup so hard that some of it spilled over the edge and sizzled with a burning smell on the black iron range. Gerry's safe, she thought, and you're safe, and soon you'll be going away from this valley of death down into the high prairie, and soon after that all these will be names, oh, you'll feel sorry all right, but the reality will go away, because you can't deal with so much death all at once, all in one morning.

"I've got to tell Ruby and Tom about their mother," she said to the soup pot, and whipped off the apron she'd been wearing. Mrs. Bell had no objection.

"But if you can come back later, dear, we could sure use the help. Mr. Bell is getting the stuff ready for a big stew."

Up in the room in the Frank Hotel, there were no Watkins children, just a note:

> Dear Miss Freeman,
>
> Our Mama is alive, and at the doctor's. Fernie is also alive, not hurt at all. She is at a friend of Mama's over the other side of town, and we are going there. Thanks for the clothes.
>
> Ruby Watkins
>
> PS: Da's in the mine. We're praying.

Mr. Manual was at the desk when she came through the lobby again. "Oh, Mr. Manual, is it all right to use the room another night? I don't know exactly how long …"

"Don't worry Miss Freeman, as long as you like. Your brother is working with the rescue gangs over t' the flats, did you know?"

"Yes, and if he comes, tell him I'm working over at the Palm. And if people ask, Mrs. Bell has quite a list of people who are safe, some hurt and some …"

"Dead. I know. It's an awful sad day. Many good people, and so many children." He looked over her shoulder. "Go right ahead up, Lillian. Second room on the right. I'll ask my wife to look in on you in a few minutes."

Laura turned to see Lillian Clark at the bottom of the stairs, clutching a pillowcase full of something. "Lillian! I thought you were … I mean, I heard…"

A stricken face looked back at her. "Laura. They're gone. Ma, and all. Just gone. And Dad's somewhere in the mine, they think. They needed the room at the boarding house and said Mr. Manual would put me up. And…" The thin face suddenly opened up into a wail, the tight lines in the cheeks a pure white, the forehead scarlet, and just a thin keening note coming out, almost too high to hear. The pillowcase fell to the floor. Laura rushed to comfort her, and Mr. Manual came out from behind the desk.

"Poor kid. She worked late at the boarding house, and they told her she might as well sleep over there. Now there's people calling her lucky. Don't think it's lucky myself." He picked up the pillowcase and started up the stairs. Laura kept her arm around Lillian and steered her up the stairs, the thin high wail continuing with hardly a break. Mr. Manual held a door open, and she brought Lillian through it, to the bed. The girl's moan broke into crying. Laura gently pushed her back to rest on the pillow, and her body obeyed, but her arms kept one of Laura's hands trapped against her chest. Laura swivelled to sit on the bed, and nodded to Mr. Manual.

His face grim, the hotel owner nodded back and stepped into the hall, gently closing the door behind him.

Here I am, she thought. To Lillian I must seem like Mrs. Bell was to me, though we're the same age, practically. How horrible, your whole family, poor tyke. Well, I don't think you're up to serving soup, so it's here we'll stay, for a while anyway. The girl's arms were relaxing, but she didn't move her hand. Maybe she'll sleep, it's the only thing, there's nothing I can say. And then the face relaxed too, and Lillian was asleep.

After fifteen minutes, she eased her weight from the bed, and Lillian slept on. The window looked out on Turtle Mountain, but the next building cut off any direct view of the place where the mine tipple had been. The scar on the mountain was huge, looking like the gleam of a split piece of firewood, a giant slash of white against the darkness of the mountain.

There was a writing desk and a chair near the window, and she thought of her parents. Normally she wrote them a long letter every Sunday, detailing the entire week, but she had not written this week, saving things for her arrival—why she would have been there long before now! She slid out of the door and down the stairs. Mr. Manual was glad to supply her with an ink pot, a pen, and some paper. This would be different, more formal than her pencilled regular letters, but the magnitude of the disaster made it seem right.

> Dear Mother and Father,
>
> First of all, if this should reach you before I do, Gerry and I are both completely all right. You know that his house and shop are right in the middle of the slide area, but he suggested the day before that we should spend the night in town, and so we were in the Frank Hotel when the slide came down shortly after four A.M. He's out working with rescue teams, and I'm taking care of

a poor young girl whose whole family was killed. Right now, I don't know when it will be possible to leave Frank and go home, but when I do, I'm going to insist that Gerry come too.

How can I describe what Frank is like now? I'm looking out over the slide, and I would guess it's about three miles wide. The rocks rolled or slid halfway up the north side of the valley, so that they came to rest about five hundred feet higher than the town, and perhaps four miles from where they started. So, from Gold Creek east, there is about twelve square miles of the most awful desolation.

Many have died. Gerry's shop was just about the farthest out of any dwellings, except a couple of ranch houses, and I cannot say whether they were struck. But Gerry's place is totally buried under at least twenty feet of rock. A mile east from his place, there was a construction camp for the railway, but I have no idea how many were sleeping there last night.

Closer in to the town, there were a number of houses that I used to pass each day, walking to the Sanatorium. One was the Warringtons' house. I told you about Florence and her plans to go to Ontario. How I wish she had gone last week! The whole family is dead, I fear. Mr. Warrington was not at home, but working in the coal mine, but this is no comfort, for the whole shift (twenty men, I'm told) are sealed in, cut off from the world. if they are alive at all. No one seems to know if there was an explosion in the mine or not.

> There is no sign of the livery stable. I heard that the body of Francis Rochette was found <u>on</u> <u>top</u> of the slide rocks, almost unmarked, but dead. He was a cheerful young man who always had a happy good morning for me.

She paused in her writing. She had seen Frank Rochette only yesterday, but her most vivid memory of him was from the week before, when she and Burt were hunting crocuses. The crocuses would be crushed now, too.

Would there ever be crocuses again over that expanse? Probably, for there would be bits of dirt. Back to the letter.

> There were some other houses there, one just recently occupied by some miners just over from England I don't know if they were on the evening shift, but if they were, I hope they followed the example of a man I met this morning, who didn't go to bed, but just caroused in town all night.
>
> Closest in to town was a row of miners' cottages. Of the six, I believe five were occupied, and of those I knew three families. The Clarks, sadly, all perished except for the poor girl sleeping on the bed in the room where I am writing this. Her whole family gone, and her father who is in the mine, alive or dead. She herself stayed in town, totally by chance, like Gerry and me.
>
> Another family, the Watkins, were dealt with more luckily, I suppose, though Mrs. Watkins is evidently badly hurt. All three children survived (Gerry and I pulled the two oldest from the creek!) The father, again, was on the shift in the mine, and his fate is not known.

The Leitch family I have not heard about. Their cottage was second in the row, counting from the creek, and it may be that it was just pushed aside by the mud that seemed to go ahead of the rock. I did see one roof there this morning that seemed intact. However, there was also a fire in that area.

I suppose any occurrence like this brings out the best and the worst in people. This morning, on the main street of Frank, one can see as many as ten or twelve men roaring drunk. But there are also heroes. I understand a salesman from Ottawa was one of the first across the creek to begin rescuing survivors, and I expect he's still there. A railway brakeman (I think his name is Shawcutt—that's what it sounded like) went across the rubble of the slide when it had barely stopped moving, and was successful in flagging down the Spokane Flyer before it crashed into the rocks. He said (I hear, because I've never met the man) that the rocks were hot to the touch from their wild ride down the mountain, and so sharp that his boots are cut to ribbons.

Quieter heroes and heroines as well. Mrs. Bell, of the Palm Restaurant has been feeding people all day from the goodness of her heart. I've got to get back to help her soon. The doctor has been working on the injured since dawn. And there are teams of miners who have crossed the floodwaters (both the river and the creek have been dammed by the slide) to try to force their way into the mine and rescue their comrades.

Poor Lillian is sleeping quite soundly now. I'll ask Mrs. Manual to check on her. Time to feed the hungry. I'll finish this later.

    She slipped from the room and went to the one she and Gerry had slept in. Opening her case to slide the unfinished letter in, she felt two other envelopes—Burt's letters that she was going to mail in Pincher Creek. What was she to do with them? She had the feeling that the one to Minneapolis was a bitter one, and wondered if it was right to send it. But could it be right not to? She couldn't think of this right now, she couldn't start thinking about one more person possibly dead. She would talk to Mrs. Manual and go to the restaurant. Try to do some good.

Chapter 9

He was riding swiftly across dry prairie, Montana, with the long rolls of hills turning blue in the distance. Although his horse was galloping powerfully, there was no shock or sensation of the hooves meeting the ground. He rolled in the saddle, as he would in a ride like this, but no pounding could be felt; it was as if the horse was running on a cushion of air just above the ground. And there was no sound of hooves, just a steady thumping coming from somewhere, and his own breathing, long sighing breaths.

"Yer turn next, Delaney." The sunlit prairie faded and darkened. A hand clutched his shoulder and a body half sat, half fell beside him. "Don't know when we'll just have to give this idea up."

Another voice hissed. "Save your breath, you fool. Use it for work."

Burt got to his feet and staggered, catching himself with a hand against the unseen wall of coal. His legs were wobbly, and his chest hurt. He knew he was breathing deeply, he could feel his chest moving, but it was as if there was nothing coming in. To the left, he thought, and felt his way along. The thumping was the rhythmic sound of a pick, and there was the dry rustle of falling coal, mixed with the whooshing sound of the shovel dragging it away. Burt met the shoveller, sensing the man's presence from a foot or two away. "I'll take over." There were no thanks, just a hand grasping his arm and a shovel pushed into his chest.

Fifteen men working. Joe Chapman had insisted on joining the work crews when one man passed out ... when? About an hour ago, maybe. But there weren't really fifteen men working now, more like seven or eight. The rest were in various states of stupor. Burt began the listless sweep of the narrow tunnel with his shovel. No lights now. There wasn't enough air to keep a lamp alight, and if there were, there were lungs that needed it more. Burt had no idea where the coal he was moving back was ending. Probably he was burying the legs of some men slumped against the wall as he had been, but it didn't matter. As long as there was that "chunk chunk" of picks ahead of him, there was a chance, and the tunnel behind the two workers at the face had to be kept clear.

"Who's up there?" he asked in a choked whisper between picks hitting the face.

"Dan."

"John ... Watkins."

"Burt Delaney here. Need someone to spell you?"

The picks fell silent. The two men were thinking. Then Dan said, "No, it's alright for a while." and the rhythm started again. Burt knew they were as tired as he was, and knew they had done more than anyone else. It wasn't fair, but fair had ceased to count. If those two retreated from the face, it was possible that no one could force himself up there to replace them. It was like a rubber band stretched to its limit. If you relaxed and let it go, then tried to stretch it again, it would probably break before it reached full length. He resumed the blind sweeps with his shovel.

Suddenly, there was a grunt from above. "Through, by God!" It was Dan's voice again. Burt heard the pick being worked loose, and a shaft of light burst into the tunnel, momentarily blinding him. The next sensation was a rush of cold air past him. He stood there and gulped it in, his lungs feeling there was something in the air for the first time in hours. He felt almost drunk instantly.

Then a jumble of voices came from behind him, the words mingling, many words that would be considered curses in the world outside, but which were uttered with the reverence of a monk on his deathbed. Dan's pick worked some more, and the shaft of light widened, the river of air grew stronger. Burt backed down the tunnel over the loose coal. As he emerged into the larger chamber, now lit by the light from the tunnel, he saw men starting to get up. It looked like something he remembered from a fairy tale — was it Aunt Jo, or was it his mother, maybe even his father? — anyway it was about an enchanted castle where everybody goes to sleep wherever he was, whatever he was doing, and then, years later, the spell is lifted and they all come to life. The men were stretching, he felt himself yawn, and he had the sense of being in the world again, even in this dim chamber.

Someone came past him. Dan McKenzie. If things were right, Burt thought, these men would be lining up and saluting the man who had brought the outside world back to them. But things are never right to that extent, and all that happened was Dan finding Joe Chapman. "Joe, you better come look. We're out, that's true, but she's some sight out there. Don't stick your head out, there's a bunch of stuff coming from above, almost lost my head to a chunk of loose size of a football, came skipping down.

"John still up there?"

"Sure. He's being careful. If you and me go up there, I've got an idea. I took a peek, kinda between rocks, and there's an overhang. Looks like the seam might go over there. Come and have a look."

Ten minutes later, the plan was settled. To widen Dan's air hole would be useless, for there was no ledge to stand on, and rocks were bounding past every few seconds. But there was a spot, thirty or forty feet up, and slightly to their left that looked like their own seam come to the surface again. Burt had no idea how far they had come to get to the air now, but thirty or forty feet more seemed like nothing to men breathing fresh air. And it was done in little more than an hour. Seventeen men, one of them on a litter, emerged to shelter under some huge boulders which had landed on the mountainside and half buried themselves.

Burt was the sixth or seventh man out. As he was hauling himself erect, Dan shouted, "Halloo!" A shout answered from below. There were a dozen men down there, a little to their left. They had picks and shovels, but all were looking up at the group of miners under the overhanging boulders. Then the men below started scrambling up the slope towards them.

The sun was already low in the west, but its slanting rays made the wide carpet of white limestone shine. It covered the entire valley. Burt could see a narrow lake extending up where Gold Creek should be, and everything to the right of that was desolation, from the mud streaks to the shining limestone going up the far side of the valley, higher than the spot where the emerging miners perched under their sheltering boulders. Where there should have been a river, some fields and trails, a railway, even where there should have been a cemetery with small evenly spaced stones, there was a mass of rock, blocks of stone small and large, tossed in a random heap, none of the blocks looking like they had inscriptions for those who lay below.

Burt looked around at his fellow survivors. All of them had come out, he thought, with wide grins, greeting open air, sunlight, and life again, with joy. But now he could see the consternation in many faces. John Watkins was staring at the place where his house should have been. William Warrington, whose leg was almost certainly broken, and who had not made one sound of pain all day, took one look at the field of rock covering his home, and howled.

Then the first group of rescuers from below were among them, and the whole group walked, slid, stumbled to the place where the adit had been. Joe Chapman looked around and asked, "Any sign of the tipple?"

"Some timbers, some steel, not much else."

"Then Tashigan's gone. Clark and Farrington were out here. Did they get away?"

"We found Fred Farrington's body, came floating up when the river flooded. No sign of Alex Clark. Was he out here for sure?"

"Here or in the part of the drift that collapsed. No hope for him, then. Other than those three, the whole shift got out, only Will Warrington hurt bad."

The dammed river was flowing over the slide, broken into a hundred rivulets picking their way past rocks, spread over a hundred yards wide. A raft ferry had been rigged on the west side of the dam, and the maintenance shift miners were taken across in three loads. Warrington was on the first ferry, but before he had gotten aboard he had received the news, his whole family gone. Burt stood beside John Watkins as they watched the group being hauled across a lake that hadn't been here the night before. "My kids are all safe," Watkins said. "The wife's gotten hurt some, I hear. God, did you ever see anything like it?"

"Never. Never again, I hope."

"Must be a hundred people under that. About four, wasn't it, when it happened?"

"Few minutes past. We were in there over thirteen hours. I think my mining days are over, John."

"Smart lad. For you, anyway. But a lot of us miners, y'know, we figure if you get past a big bump, you're kind of safe for life, like you got a spell or a charm or something. I'm not saying I'm going back mining, but you never know." He looked up the mountain. "They'll have to be pretty hungry for coal to get this one going again, though."

The ferry was rigged from bridge timbers and a long rope loop. Four big men operated it, holding the rope and walking toward the stern, then peeling off and picking up the rope again at the bow. Karl Grafton was one, and as he brushed past Burt, he said, "Welcome back to the world." The next time it was, "This open air work's not bad." Then "May get into the ferry business full time." Each time, Burt prepared himself to answer, but Karl was always past him before he could. Then the raft bumped against the ground at the end of Dominion Avenue.

As they walked up Dominion, there were brilliant flashes from both sides of the street. "Photographers," said Shorty, "and me without me hair combed." A wagon went ahead, pulled by eager men, taking William Warrington to the doctor's house. John Watkins had hurried ahead to catch up to it. People detached themselves from the lined sidewalks to rush out and meet miners thought dead all day.

Laura didn't rush out, but Burt saw her waving with a bouncing urgency, and he swerved off the line of march to meet her. She fairly jumped at him, and hugged him so hard he almost staggered back into the street. "Oh, Burt, we were so worried, so scared. It's been awful here, so many people killed, and then we thought you and your, the men on your shift, why nobody's even dared to hope, and then the news came that you were out, at least most of you, and … well, it's the first good news all day in this place, that's what it seems … and how are you, anyway?"

With this she leaned back and looked up at him. She was wearing a long apron over her dress, and that had gotten pretty dirty from his mine clothes, but her face was what he saw first. The whole left side was black from his shirt. All he could do was laugh.

She looked startled. "What's wrong, I mean, we had a right to be worried…"

"Not that, Laura. Your face. My shirt is pretty dirty."

She wiped her cheek with one hand and looked at her fingers. Then she smiled, perhaps the most beautiful sight he had seen in his life. "Is that all?" She leaped at him again, and again he staggered back. When she finished hugging him this time, she wiped her right cheek. "Do I match now?" He nodded , and they turned to follow the line of miners and families up the street.

"Is Gerry all right?"

"Yes, tired, and he'll probably be working more tonight, but it's looking pretty hopeless out there. I think they've found a few people just hurt, and about ten bodies, but it's not easy. Gerry's such a gentle person, did you know that?" He squeezed her hand

and nodded. "It's been hard on him. Once he found a leg. Nothing more. He didn't want to talk about it, but some reporter was asking him and asking him, and I think Gerry was almost ready to hit the man. Those reporters will be wanting to talk to the men on your shift. Stay out of the bars."

He laughed. "I'm not much for bars, Laura. But some of the guys are probably in one by now, and they'll be talking plenty."

"What was it like in there, Burt?"

"Up to the bump, normal. Then the problem was air, and that was a pretty close thing. We dug up because going through the adit was completely impossible. Got through to air, and none too soon, it was getting pretty stale in there. Dark, too, we couldn't keep lamps going."

She stopped and twirled. "No light? None at all?"

"Had to work by feel, the last bit."

"Burt, I would have died! How could you stand it?"

"When you don't have a choice, you don't have a choice. I think a couple of fellows in there were about to choose dying, but I didn't want to. And neither did most, there were some real heroes there, Laura. But I guess I've got a choice now, and I think I've worked in my last mine. But I'll draw my pay."

It was twilight, and lanterns were winking on. Burt looked down the street and said, "Seem's everybody's out tonight. Look, isn't that Gerry?" Gerry was on the sidewalk in front of the Palm Restaurant.

"That's him! Are you hungry, Burt? Well, for heaven's sake you must be and you must think me a fool for even asking! Let's go, Mr. Bell and I have been working together, um, collaborating, is that the word, on a *magnificent* stew. He adds stuff and I stir, and believe me, he's added at least one cow and a whole field of potatoes. And I've stirred up a storm. Hi, there, Gerry! Are you hungry. Look who I dug up!"

"And dragged home. Glad to see you, Gerry."

"Not half as glad as we are to see you! And the whole town. You know, when the news went around that you fellows were out of the mountain, it was the first good news all day. You could look around and see people look up for the first time and hope that things would get better, like a mountain had landed on their spirits, and now they could think of shaking it off."

Inside the Palm, Mrs. Bell hurried up some slow eaters so they could have a table. Laura started for the kitchen but was stopped. "You sit right down there with your brother and your young man!" Burt heard, and looked intently at Laura and the older woman. Laura turned, looking embarrassed, but then looked straight in his eyes, set her mouth firm, and smiled. She looked back at Mrs. Bell.

"Can I wash my face a bit?"

This brought a hoot of laughter. "Honest coal dust, girl. But go ahead." Laura disappeared into the kitchen. When she got back to the table, Gerry grinned up at her.

"Do you want to sit beside me, or beside your young man?"

Now she was annoyed and amused at the same time. "With my young man, thank you very much!" She sat down quickly in the chair beside Burt.

A bowl of stew was put before Gerry, who looked up at Mrs. Bell. Burt leaned towards Laura and said, quickly and quietly, "Thank you. It's a compliment."

She looked straight ahead. "The young man statement?"

"Yes. I can't think of anything better that you could say. I mean, I'd like to be."

"This is too fast, you know that."

It was, he did realize it was. It was just that she was like that rush of air down the tunnel, the one that had made him feel alive again. "You're right. No more, not now. But I have an idea in my head, Miss Laura Freeman, that the time will come when you'll say 'my young man' and mean it."

Gerry was looking at them now. She turned to Burt and asked, "Where will you be staying tonight?"

"I expect in his own room." Gerry put in. "We have the greater problem. His building is still standing."

"Oh, Gerry, did you talk with Mr. Manual? I mentioned to him that…"

"That we'd need the room another night? Yes, we spoke. And, by the way, I got to the telegraph and relayed through Cranbrook that we're safe and unhurt. To the parents, you know."

"Gerry, I'll have you know that I met Sergeant Ross, you know, the Pincher Creek detachment, and he relayed the very same message. So there. I at least am writing a letter to explain things more fully. You might try that idea some time."

"Defeated, I address my stew." All three ate, Burt realizing for the first time how hungry he was. And tired.

Then a thought struck him. "Laura, did you… I mean, those letters I gave you, are they …?"

"No, still in my case. I worried about them when I was putting my own letter in, and I thought you, well I didn't know if you'd ever come out of that mine. I was actually thinking of just destroying them. Is that awful? I mean, I'd have no right, but it seemed to me from what you said that it wouldn't be good for them to go if you were, maybe, not there. Do you see what I was feeling?"

"I'm just glad they're not gone., I did some thinking today, and most of it was about how I wasn't thinking too straight before. I'll get the letters from you when it's handy. There's something in one of them I should retrieve, to save a bit of money."

She looked puzzled, so he added, "Don't worry, I'll explain later. I'm going to have another bowl of stew. I missed lunch."

They both walked him back to the boarding house. "As soon as we know we can get a train on the other side of the slide, Gerry and I are going down to Pincher Creek. Why don't you come and visit for a little while? Meet my parents." He was sure she was smiling at him in the dark.

"Yes, I will. There's nothing to keep me in Frank. And I have to go east anyway, there's a few things I have to do."

83

As he went in, he felt light. The things he had to do were clear in his mind now, and so were many other things.

Chapter 10

August in Macleod was always dusty, and this summer had been even drier than usual. Laura wore a riding skirt, boot length, so the dust didn't bother her as much as it did the ladies who opted for finery when they came to Macleod for the market and fair. Da was looking for a good bull at a fair price. She and Mum had done their shopping yesterday, and this morning she had finished her other business, the purchase of six hides for Gerry. The hides would be rolled and shipped to him in Blairmore, she'd been promised.

Gerry's new shop in Blairmore was flourishing. Although they'd allowed the people of Frank to return to their homes (many, of course, had never left) a couple of weeks after the slide, very few of those who had moved returned, for the mine was not reopened immediately. Gerry had followed his customers to Blairmore, and was as busy as he cared to be.

The mine entrance had been opened on May 30th, just over a month after the slide. The workers were amazed to find a horse alive in there. "It was Charley," Gerry's letter explained, "who stayed alive by chewing wood. The water had not reached that level, and there must have been enough air coming in from the escape tunnel. He was pretty gaunt by the time they got to him, and very weak. They practically carried him out and took him to town, the last hero of the famous Frank Slide. Unfortunately, he was also the last casualty, for the damn fools fed him oats and brandy, and the poor beast died. Tell Burt, if you're writing to him." Gerry's letter was characteristically tardy.

Laura had written the news to Burt, care of Mr. James Delaney, General Delivery, Minneapolis, but hadn't received a reply yet, though it had been over a month. He had stayed with them in Pincher Creek for four days at the beginning of May. Then he used the ticket his father had sent and which he had intended to send back. "I'm pretty sure I'm not staying there," he'd said, "but I do have to talk with him. I think I can see how he thought he was in a tight place ten years ago. I'd like to think I'd never do what he did, but maybe I have to be more ... more conscious of *why*. And I want to see my sister Laura very much." In late June, he'd written, and again in early July. Since then, nothing.

This was the house, she was sure. The sign was there, "Rooms with Board", and it was at the address she'd seen on the letter to Jo, Mrs. Jo Garrity. Standing looking up at the house, she felt foolish. She should just go back to the fair grounds and meet her mother. The house was big and square, shiplap lumber on the outside, and regular rows of windows indicating lots of bedrooms, at least upstairs. While she was standing in the dust of the street, a boy came out, a pail in one hand, and a long stick with a mop in the other. He looked at her curiously, then moved to a position below the first window on the second floor. He dipped the mop in the pail, then stretched on tiptoe to reach the top of the window, swirling it back and forth in a quick twisting motion. The window dripped water, making streaks on the shiplap boards. By the time the water was making mud in the dust, the boy was on to the next window.

Laura studied him. This would be Jimmy. His hair was lighter than Burt's. He looked about ten or eleven, which would be right. She would not have picked him out on the street as Burt's brother, but here, with the expectation of meeting him, she could see the resemblance. He was thin, but would probably fill out when he was fifteen or so.

By now, he had finished the second window on the second floor and was about to move around the corner of the house. Between each movement, he glanced at her. She had better do something, either go up to the door, or go away. She breathed deeply, and walked up to the door.

Her knock got no immediate reply, and she was about to knock again when the door opened abruptly in front of her raised hand. The woman in front of her didn't look a bit like Burt: she was square, sturdily built, about five feet three, with a broad, flat face. She wore an apron so big it almost brushed her feet, tied with a long string at the front , with bows a foot long. Her face looked stiff, almost grim. Laura said, "I'm sorry…" and stopped.

The grim visage dissolved into a huge smile. "Sorry for what, dear? I should be the one to be sorry, but I thought it was one of those pesky little rascals who are always after Jimmy to play, and him with work to do. He'll be finished in an hour and they know that, but they still persist in askin' when. Now, what can I do for you?" The beam in the face was so strong that Laura felt she could ask for a three course meal and her wish would be granted.

"You'd be Mrs. Jo Garrity?" A nod, and the beam continued. "My name is Laura Freeman. I'm a friend of…" She was interrupted by a cry of welcome and two arms folding her into the huge apron.

"Of course you are! As if Burt hadn't described you to the life! Come in, come in. Ain't it hot out? Dusty, too, and I guess you'd like some cool water. That right? Here, sit down, sit down. This is the parlour, and I'll be the maid today, for our regular one is off." She winked and grinned. "Seventeen years she's been gone, but I fill in." Laura sat on the edge of the chair as Jo Garrity bustled into the hall and disappeared into the kitchen. What to say next?

She'd rehearsed this all the way down from Pincher Creek to Macleod. No offence, and I have no real right to know, but is Burt Delaney staying in the east? Have you heard from him? It's just that I thought … well, I thought he wanted to know me better, that he would be coming back this way. Now if he's not going to visit us again, could you give him my very best regards?

Jo Garrity came back into the room. "And how is Burt? Did his trip east agree with him? I'll give him what-for for not seeing us on the way through, but I guess he took the fastest route. Well, what did he find out there?"

Laura's mouth was open to ask her first question, but all she could do was breathe out. Then in again. "He didn't come here?"

"Course not, dear. Last I heard, he was heading out into Columbia, but going through the States. But he was writing about seeing you, first thing he could. Surely he wrote the same thing to you?"

Laura shook her head, then sipped the water Jo had handed to her. "No, not a word for over five weeks. He wrote me from Minneapolis when he got there, and then once more. Maybe he changed his mind?"

"That boy change his mind? That'd be like the Rocky Mountains changing their shape." Laura winced. She had seen Turtle Mountain change its shape, and the effects were stronger than Jo Garrity imagined when she used the comparison. "No, dear, he wrote to me and Jimmy ... did you see Jimmy outside?"

"Yes, but we didn't speak."

"Right. He's a good boy, doing his chores like I told him. Anyway, Burt wrote, oh well, I guess it would be almost five weeks ago. He was coming west, but going straight to this valley he wanted to see. Then he said by September, he'd have a plan."

That was all the information she got out of Jo Garrity. Oh, she was told more about Burt's youth than he'd want her to know, and about the other Laura, who Jo was sure was perfect, and about Jo's brother, James, who was not perfect, but was a brother, you know. Jo seemed to assume that Burt was engaged to her, Laura Freeman, or practically so. Jo also assumed that Laura was completely happy about joining the Delaney-Garrity family, and she took Laura's growing redness of complexion as proof of this.

"Well, dear, keep in touch. General Delivery will get me here. I'm sure you'll find a letter waiting at home. Don't worry, that Burt has never let anyone down. It's not in him."

As the door closed, Laura almost yelled out into the street, but she breathed hard and walked quickly towards the fairgrounds. She had never been so embarrassed. Here she was, *counting* on him, and he was all over the country, not even letting her know! She walked so fast that two people she passed looked back at her and the dust she was raising. At the fairgrounds, her mother took one look at her and pursed her lips. Nothing was asked. Nothing was offered. The only words Laura said were, "Is Da ready? It will take us forever to get home."

There was only one good thing. She hadn't told her mother that she was going to visit Burt's aunt. Her mother might guess, but she wouldn't pry. Laura forced herself to chat, to ask about her mother's purchases, as the wagon rolled slowly towards Pincher Creek, a big white-faced bull trailing behind with a rope through its nose ring. The wagon had several months supply of coffee, tea, spices, sugar, as well as many yards of cotton and linen for the family's clothing for the coming year. Normally, she would be looking forward to the unpacking, to see the colours her mother had chosen, but today, she just felt dull and sad. It wasn't that she had any claim on Burt, no matter what his aunt thought. It was just that he'd promised to keep in touch, and he hadn't.

The bull was not a fast walker, and Da didn't want to hurt him. For a long time they were heading right into the sun, enlarging itself as it sank toward the mountains. Then there was the long late summer twilight, and finally the stars winking on as the glow faded in the west. It would be cold tonight, maybe even some frost up home. The creak of the wagon harness, the breathing of the horses ahead and the bull behind, formed a background to the sharper sounds of coyotes out on the prairie. She made herself comfortable against a bolt of cloth, and slept.

She woke suddenly. The wagon had stopped, and they were home. Gerry was there, beside the wagon, holding a lantern high. Behind him was Burt Delaney.

"What are you doing here?"

"Well, I know I'm a day late, but I gather that if I had gotten here yesterday like I promised, you wouldn't have been here. But it doesn't matter. What's a day?"

Promised? "When did you promise? And what?"

"I wrote three weeks ago, saying I'd be here August twenty-first, Friday. That I'd try to see Gerry up in the pass on my way, because I'd be coming from the west. Didn't you get the letter?"

So that was it. "Where did you send it from?"

"A fellow I knew was going up valley to a place called Revelstoke. It's on the main CPR line. He said he'd mail it there."

"I saw your aunt today, down in Macleod. She said you were going west, but I thought you'd just forgotten to tell us."

Gerry broke in. "Enough of this talking out here in the dark. Let's go, Laura, so I can help unload the wagon. Inside, the two of you, and argue there."

"It's all right, Gerry." As she said this, she realized that it was all right. "Here, this goes to the back room, on the top shelf." A huge bolt of cloth was handed to Burt. "And this with it." Gerry got his bundle, which he had to flip under one arm to keep the lantern. Laura turned back to the wagon. It wouldn't do to let either of them see the tears on her cheeks.

Gerry had coffee brewed and a cold supper out on the table. Within a half hour, Da had the bull in a stall, and the horses unhitched and fed. Sure enough, her mother wanted the flowers covered, and they all worked for a few minutes spreading burlap over makeshift supports. Then they were ready for the food and coffee.

Burt held their attention. "It's every bit as good as I'd heard. There's a chain of lakes in the valley, and I've got an option on some land down toward the south end, ten, fifteen miles from the

US line. I've been working a bit for a rancher near there, getting the hang of things. He says the winters are really mild, no problem for stock at all, and the lakes hardly ever even freeze over. Anyway, I've got permission to build on the land I'm planning on buying, and I'll be going back out there as soon as I've visited Aunt Jo and Jimmy. The rancher can use me right over the winter, and in my spare time, I'll put a cabin up. Then, in the spring, I'll buy the land, and get some yearlings. It'll be a couple of years to get the place going, but it will be good, I'll tell you."

"Water?" Da was a man of few words.

"A good creek right through it, even a spot where I can put a weir and start a line to a pond. There's some good timber, too, in the higher part, enough for a barn and outbuildings."

"But how can you ... I mean, you were going to have to save another year or more, and then the slide came. How can you manage it now?" Laura thought things were going awfully quickly.

"Well, my father decided to lend me the start-up money. Wanted to give it to me, but we settled on a long term loan. I'm not worried. There's lots of mining in the area, a big gold strike up the Similkameen River at a place called Hedley. Mining south of the border too, and it's a lot drier down there. The market for beef will be good."

It was after midnight when her mother's yawns were too frequent to ignore. Laura said she wanted to check on Ginger down in the barn, and Burt offered to go with her.

"How was it?" she asked, "I mean, with your father and all. Maybe you said in the letter."

"Not everything. It was pretty stiff at first. He was ... I guess you'd say cautious. At first, he kept talking about me going into the store, well, the second store he's planning on opening. Minneapolis is getting very big now, and he's got a really good business going. I finally convinced him that it wouldn't happen, that ranching is something I'm going to do no matter what, and then he offered me the money. He said he'd probably have spent more than that on my education, and since I'd done that part myself, I deserved it. But we settled on the loan."

"What about his ... your step-mother?"

"Grace?" He laughed. "For ten years, I've built that woman up as the great enemy. She's not, not really. She's actually scared stiff of me, as if she thinks I'm going to hit her or something. She does love him, I can see that, and she loves Laura, too. It must be that for the last ten years, she's been building up a picture of me, too. That I'm going to come and take my revenge. It's probably as much relief for her as for me that I'm going to live in the west."

Ginger snickered to see Laura, and she and Burt petted the mare as they talked. "My sister's thirteen now, and she's part of that family, and Minneapolis. It wouldn't be doing her a favour to bring her away, even if I could. But she was really interested when I told her about Laura Freeman out west, the heroine of the Frank Slide."

"Away with you! You didn't say that!"

"No, but I did tell her that I thought you were the nicest person I'd ever met. And I do."

She wasn't sure how to respond. "We're still pretty young, Burt."

"I'm eighteen now, and soon to be an independent rancher. And you're seventeen. That was in my letter, too, best wishes on your birthday. And I'm not talking about anything immediate. But next year, about this time, I'll be coming through here again, and I'd like it if we could ... well decide on our future together, that is, if we have a future together. What do you think, Laura?"

"Well. I suppose that ... if I say yes, I'm not really saying yes to anything but you coming around next year, right?"

"I think I love you, Laura."

"I think I love you, too, Burt. And I think next year it will be the same. But don't talk to Gerry about it, not yet. He's an awful tease."

He blew out the lantern after they closed the barn door, and they walked hand in hand to the ranch house under the high, cold stars.

Printed in Canada